JULIEN PARME

FLORIAN ZELLER

JULIEN PARME

Translated from the French
by Christopher Moncrieff

PUSHKIN PRESS
LONDON

English translation © Christopher Moncrieff 2008

First published in French as
Julien Parme © Flammarion 2006

This edition first published in 2008 by
Pushkin Press
12 Chester Terrace
London N1 4ND

British Library Cataloguing in Publication Data:
A catalogue record for this book is available
from the British Library

ISBN 978 1 901285 97 0

Cover: *Untitled* Bill Henson 2003
Courtesy of the Artist Roslyn Oxley9 Gallery Sydney
& Robert Miller Gallery New York

Frontispiece: Florian Zeller 2006
© Arnaud Février Flammarion

Set in 10.5 on 13.5 Monotype Baskerville
and printed in the United Kingdom
by T J International

For Gabriel

For now he thought it convenient and necessary, as well for the increase of his own honour, as the service of the public, to turn knight-errant, and roam through the whole world, armed cap-à-pie *and mounted on his steed, in quest of adventures; that thus imitating those knights-errant of whom he had read, and following their course of life, redressing all manner of grievances, and exposing himself to danger on all occasions, at last, after a happy conclusion of his enterprises, he might purchase everlasting honour and renown.*

Don Quixote
CERVANTES

PART ONE

PREPARATIONS

1

At the risk of surprising you I'd like to tell you about the incredible thing that happened to me last year. Not that I'm bragging, but things like that, I swear to you, things as incredible as what I'm going to tell you, they don't happen every day. They never happen, even. That's why I'm talking about it. Because me, I'm not the sort to yak on to people about my life. Question of style. Like this guy who was in my class at the time, Antoine Cheval he was called. A fucker of a name when you think about it. Well, you'd ask him a question, anything, just polite like, so at least he'd have the impression he existed and everything, and that was it, he'd rabbit on to you for hours all about himself. That sort of person has always made me want to puke. That's why if someone says he's got an incredible thing to tell you, I'd be more the sort to be wary, because someone who says that, you shouldn't give him the chance to go any further. Never. Otherwise you're forced to listen to him to the end, and then, well, you might just say you're stuffed.

But in my case it's not the same, seeing it's me who's doing the telling, and I'm not Antoine Cheval. With him, I let myself be taken in at first. To be friendly I gave him all that 'where are you from' and 'what do you think about it'. But basically I couldn't give a toss. It's just that we sat next to each other in class. I was new, seeing I'd only just arrived from Paris. Right in the middle of the school year as well. I'd been fooling around a bit back there, and they'd sent me to this rubbish town in the East. A sort of punishment, like.

13

I haven't told you yet that my mother was slightly steamed up. I ought to have started there. Because she was *really* steamed up. Like all mothers, you'll tell me. Except that she was even more steamed up than a normally steamed-up mother. Mega-strict, no sense of humour, nothing. You couldn't have a joke with her. So I often got a bollocking, obviously. Frankly it was no fun. But now when I think about it, I tell myself that in fact it was quite the opposite: she wasn't steamed up, my mother, she was just blown out. Like a candle in a draught.

I was living in Paris with her and François. A moron with a skimpy little beard and corduroy trousers. My father, he died of cancer when I was about nine. That's why afterwards she went with different blokes. And the latest in the long line of muppets was this François. Right. But after the stupid things I did, they wanted to send me to my uncle's in Nice. That's normal you're going to tell me, parents, it's what they're for: all I had to do was not fool around. But if you want to know the whole of it, I think it was just an excuse, my stupid behaviour. The truth is they were well glad to get rid of me. It was one less thing for them to worry about. They could have some peace. An easy life, like. In a way they must have been really glad to have to punish me. Their excuse was that I hung around with the wrong people in Paris. And on top of that I was easily led. Whatever. But no chance of negotiating. When my mother had made up her mind about something it was best not to contradict her.

Except my uncle didn't want to know. It's a shame in a way, because his place was right by the sea. You could have imagined a worse punishment. All the rooms have

a balcony. You can see Italy in the distance. Italy, that's classy. Even from a distance. But he didn't want to know. I didn't really understand why. Apparently he had quite a lot of travelling to do during the year, or something like that. Anyway, so then my mother didn't know how to get rid of me, and that's when she decided to send me to a friend of the family who lived in the Vosges. I swear to you. The Vosges. Where it rains in summer. And in winter it's worse than an ice cube down the back of your neck. Me, I didn't know the Vosges still existed. Which just goes to show you. But you're probably asking yourself: and why not Siberia while you're at it? The answer's simple: because my mother didn't know anyone there. So, you can imagine, I tried everything but she didn't want to know. Her and François, they shoved me on a train with a bag, and zoom-zoom, full steam ahead for Saint-Dié. That's how it started. Or rather: that's how it ended.

Why am I telling you all this? Oh yes, because of Antoine Cheval. When I arrived in Saint-Dié he didn't have anyone next to him in class. He was the only one without someone next to that. You'd think no one wanted to sit beside a guy like him. Although a guy like Antoine Cheval, he didn't make you want to be friends with him. That's why I ended up talking to him. Because I arrived in the middle of the year and there was only one empty seat in that fucking classroom. Depressing. He never stopped telling me about his life. It was unbearable. Especially as he always harped on about irrelevant details, like dates of birth and all that stuff. He must have thought I'd come to the Vosges just to write his biog in ten volumes. What he told me was so bloody boring it almost made me want to listen to the

15

teacher. That just shows you … He was like that, Cheval; he got carried away over nothing. Know what I saw on the TV yesterday? And gee up, he was off like a shot. Seriously. A nerd, big time.

He reminded me of François. He was another one, he was. I wonder where my mother dug him up from. In an antique shop I reckon. The only thing I knew about him was that he was a nobleman. With a 'de' in front of his name and everything. De Courtois. That seemed to be really important to him. François de Courtois. I think that's pretty stupid myself. Maybe if he had had a château or something like that. But just having a 'de' in front of your name isn't anything to get fired up about. But him, he was exactly the type to get fired up about bullshit like that. Every morning he must have looked in the mirror and told himself he had a 'de'. This bloke never stopped talking about himself. He always went and did it in front of guests, for example. No sooner had they settled themselves on the sofa in the living room than he started talking about himself, the handle to his name, his family history. It was his favourite subject. Like how he was related to some bloke who'd had his head cut off. That's no reason to take our heads off as well.

I don't understand guys like that. It destroys me. No kidding, it's too much for me: I can't play the game. But in a way the guests were pretty much forced to play the game. Seeing they were guests. They listened, nodding their heads, shifting in their seats, taking a discreet look at their watch or saying: "Hm, I see, that's amazing … " In other words they played the game. But me, I never played the game. If needs be I covered my ears. Straight up. Or I went into another room, to make it quite clear to him that I didn't give a toss about his family history. That's what I

mean when I say I want to tell you an amazing thing: I'm not the type to get fired up over a load of bullshit.

In fact the so-called friend of the family, the one who put me up in the Vosges, she was certainly one of François' family. I really couldn't see what the hell I was going to do in Saint-Dié. To begin with it was the name that I found strange more than anything. Saint-Dié. As a first name it was pathetic, Dié. Hello, can I introduce Dié! It's incredible that a mother can be so off her head to call her son Dié. Didier, that's freaky enough, but Dié … They don't get it, mothers. They've no idea what they're doing. Sometimes they even do it on purpose. Okay. But I wouldn't want to seem the type who's always complaining, especially since on that count, I mean when it comes to first names, I have to admit I was lucky. I'm called Hugues. No, I'm just kidding. I'm called Julien. With my surname that gives you Julien Parme. Style. Julien Parme, you've never heard of him? The great writer? No? Really? Because I forgot to tell you I'd like to be a great writer. Okay. For example, if I'd been called Dié, I think I'd have had to change my first name. For my books. I'd have used Julien instead. To make: Julien Parme. So everything's fine. Since that's what I'm called.

Where it actually starts is the day they shoved me on the train. All this business had made me depressed. What finished me off more than anything was the feeling that they wanted to get rid of me. My mother, then my uncle. Basically, no one wanted me under their feet. As far as they were concerned I was a hopeless case. Especially my mother; on the platform I definitely sensed she was telling herself: 'Come on, just another little effort and that'll be the end of the nightmare'. It freaked me out that she didn't

even look unhappy. You have to say in her defence that she hadn't had an easy life, my mother. Protestant education and all that. I'm won't give you the low-down on her whole life, I'll just say she'd had her share of hardships. Crummy things. My father's illness for example. That's what left her rather blown out. And unable to smile any more.

Anyway, that day, the day of the train, I found it hard to smile as well, I can tell you. I was seriously depressed. And to make sure they were aware of it, my depression, I didn't answer any of their questions. I stayed stony-faced. The heroic thing, you can't get at me. But deep down I almost wanted to blub. Careful, I'm not saying I wanted to, I'm just saying I *almost* wanted to. It's not the same thing. After all, I wasn't a kid any more. I'd soon be fifteen. In a year's time.

In any case, as far as atmosphere goes, stations have never been my thing. All those people saying goodbye and crying on each other's shoulders, it's always made me melancholy. Especially on a day like that, when it was raining and really cold. And Sunday into the bargain. I had to go to school the next day. To the only place that was prepared to take me in the middle of the year … No, frankly, it was enough to make you hang yourself in your briefs. Still, my mother had bought me a new suitcase. Ginormous and everything. With wheels. To cram all my things in. And I'd taken virtually everything. My room in Paris looked like a graveyard now. I'd applied the scorched earth policy. Because in my mind, my parents weren't ever going to see me again. That's why I'd taken as much as I could in my suitcase *grand luxe*. They didn't want me any more? Fine. I wouldn't get in their way any longer. Mind you, I wasn't planning on spending my life in Saint-Dié. No thanks. I'm not mad. I know all about the country: I went there once.

I know I'm not cut out for it. But when I got back to Paris, no way would I go knocking on their door. I'd get by. I'd make a life for myself without them. Seriously. I wouldn't be the first to do it.

That day, the day of the train, I kept telling myself it was the last time I'd see my mother. I kept repeating it to make sure I realised. To get used to the idea that it was the end of something. The first part of my life. The bowl of cherries. Anyway. At the time it upset me. Like on the day of a funeral, if you want a comparison. I could already see I was going to make it a chapter in one of my future novels. A really cruel chapter, one that makes people cry and everything. I'd call it *The Farewell*. It would be the story of a hero who decides never to go home again to get his own back on his mother for her cruelty. A gut-wrencher. One day a journalist would see the key to all my work in that. She'd come to interview me. Me with my cigar, and her, a bit intimidated, obviously. "But Monsieur Parme, is it right to say that your entire, brilliant oeuvre is prefigured in this moment of separation, described in a moving chapter which you subtly and aptly titled *The Farewell?*" And then I'd reply with something hyper-intelligent which would knock her dead. I don't know what yet, but something hyper-intelligent. Thwack! There goes another one. She'd look a bit like Madame Thomas, my French teacher. After the interview we'd have dinner and then, as always, the negotiations would continue in the horizontal position.

Madame Thomas was maybe the only teacher I was disgusted to leave behind. Because at least she knew how to make her lessons interesting. She often wore a see-through blouse. I always wondered if it wasn't to give us fantasies. When you wear see-through blouses, even only slightly

see-through, you must realise, mustn't you? Anyway, she was really beautiful. For a teacher I mean. Young and everything. She'd taken the place of the one who was supposed to have been teaching us, Monsieur Vigouse, who got very ill two weeks after the *rentrée*. A fat jerk who tried to look young by wearing cowboy boots. Two centuries behind the times, the bloke was. It was that especially that made me sad at the thought of leaving the lycée. Never seeing her again. One day she'd be reading the paper and by chance she'd come across my photo with, written underneath: '*Julien Parme, Nobel Prize at the age of twenty*'. She'd remember me. She'd be overcome. And really proud. Obviously. So she'd straightway go and buy my book in a real bookshop and she'd read it in a night to see if I mentioned her. That's how she'd realise that I'd loved her.

In my novel there would also be a pretty merciless description of François. For example, about the way this slug with a handle to his name tried to help me get my case onto the train. I told him right away it was too heavy for him. François, he was the sort of bloke who hadn't done any sport for at least fifty years. No, sixty. His whole body was dripping with sweat from doing zilch all day. I wondered what my mother saw in him, frankly. Anyway, I managed my suitcase by myself. I shoved it up on the rack. Above my seat. I made sure it wouldn't move. For safety. Because a suitcase like that could kill you if it fell on you. It's not something to joke about. Right. My mother and François were still on the platform. They were waiting for me to come back and say goodbye. I was in two minds whether to get settled into my seat, just like that, without saying anything. That would have frozen them out. Them, waiting for me on the platform and me sitting down … But all the same I thought it better to get off the train.

My mother had said she'd give me some money. No doubt I was going to need it. And besides it's not on, to not even kiss your mother when you know it's the last time you're going to see her. So I went back. Suddenly I had a vision: there they were, the pair of them, on the platform, shivering, waiting for something, and all of a sudden I got the impression they were very old, really very old, with that lost look that all old people have, the ones in wheelchairs and everything. I also got the impression they were going to die soon. And I told myself that that would be so much the better. It sent a shiver down my spine.

My mother kissed me and said she hoped this would make me think things over. You bet. François gave me a little envelope. I knew what was in it. Okay. But I still opened it. To check. There were a few notes. Almost nothing. And a letter. Fuck. I could already imagine what they'd said. Another lecture. I stuck it in my jacket pocket. It was strange, taking that money in front of them like that. After all the cash I'd pinched from them … Then François patted me on the shoulder. The typical thing from the neglectful stepfather. Then I got back on the train. I had the urge to say something pathetic like: 'Saint-Dié, it's like the bogs: when you've got to go, you've got to go!' But I refrained. I preferred to stay silent. So that right to the last minute they'd be aware just how lousy it was to send me there, to cut me off from my friends, from my life and from Mathilde.

Then there was the piercing sound of a horn. It still echoes in my mind. And the train door closed automatically.

2

I REALISE I FORGOT to tell you why they were sending me there. That's me all over. Forget to say what's important. I'll have to tell you the whole story so you can understand. Otherwise you won't understand a thing. Okay. I think you've guessed that all this was mostly down to Marc Russo. Marco to his friends. He hung out in a garret. A really nice place with a view over the rooftops and everything. His parents had bought it for him because they didn't live in Paris. To me, that was sort of my dream. The idea of living alone, no parents or anyone on your back. But I knew full well that I had a good three years to get through before then. The whole of the lycée, like. As long as I didn't have to repeat a year. Which wasn't guaranteed, since when it came to schoolwork I wasn't exactly in the habit of pushing myself too hard. Anyway. What was cool about Marco was that you could talk about anything. For example, he was pretty wised-up about girls. He'd already slept with them … Me too, obviously, but well, that's another story … So anyway. Since the *rentrée* it just happened that we were spending more and more time together. He was two years older than me. He made a speciality of re-taking years. Things must have been hanging in the balance. But not necessarily.

Up till then, in every school I'd been at I'd always been the biggest of dummies. I did fuck all. Okay. If I'd wanted I could've got good marks. But I didn't want to. For a start because I'm obstinate, and when I've decided something I don't usually change my mind. And also because I didn't

see the point. At one time I used to get really good marks. Easily, no problem. I was even one of the best in my class. And then suddenly I decided to stop. Not only to annoy my mother. But because I think they're a waste of time, good marks. That's what I told myself whenever I tried to swot up. Take maths, for example. Apart from swots who are in a hurry to wear a suit and work in an office, what use is maths? None. Take a guy who wants to be a writer: what the hell does he care if he gets nought in maths since he knows he's going to write great books and one day even his maths teacher, that turd Monsieur Ladibe for example, will be impressed to pass him in the street?

The problem was that on account of me not doing any work, my mother had got in a real rage. If you'd seen her you would have been afraid for me. As I've already told you: Protestant education and all that. It was nothing to laugh about. She said she didn't know what to do with me any more etc. That's the reason she sent me to a private school. I ought to have started there. So the story would be clearer. At the time she sent me to the *Institute*. A place where they crammed work down your throat right up to the day you took the *bac*. That's where I met Marco.

I never really liked it, that school. Actually I hated it. It was like doing military service. In fact I'm pretty sure the teachers they gave us had been recruited from the barracks. They all had their minds set on starting World War Three. No kidding. What's more it was mega-strict, no chance of having a joke or anything. At least that's what they thought. Because in actual fact we pissed around as much as people did everywhere else. And yet we heard about rules and regulations from dawn till dusk. If you didn't obey them to the letter, the rules, you got some incredible punishment. So-called. It was best to keep your nose clean there. The

only exception was Madame Thomas. She was really nice, she was. That's why I began to love French as a subject. At the start I had a really crap vocabulary. I said 'like' at the end of every sentence. And my sentences had at most three words, or four with the 'like'. Although eventually I wanted to be a writer, with cigars and interviews, and I wrote deadly essays which broke every heart in their path.

But apart from French you could have dropped dead from an overdose of boredom. I got the feeling I'd been shoved in prison. That's what I sometimes thought. For a laugh. I worked out escape plans. Seeing I was innocent. It wouldn't be long in coming. That was obvious. The moment when I'd vanish into thin air. All I had to do was be patient.

The day everything went pear-shaped, I can still remember it, I was in Marco's room—as we often were after school. But this time I was slumped in his armchair, watching him get ready. I was in a bad way. Because I was really depressed that day. For the reason that that evening, contrary to what had been planned, I wasn't going to be able to go out. Although we'd been talking about tonight for ages. The night of the year, according to Marco. Fuck. It was Émilie Fermat's birthday, a girl in her final year. A bomb, if you want to know. An atomic bomb. Who everyone fantasized about, seeing she'd already been in a film. An actress, like. I'd forgotten what the film was called, but people had been talking about it at the *Institute* every day since it came out. In the end it got on your nerves. That's why I didn't want to see it. So as not to be like the others. But later I changed my mind. When I realised she showed her breasts in the film.

But by then it just happened that the film wasn't showing any more. Anyway. Everyone had tried to get themselves invited to this birthday party.

If you were in the fifth form, like me, you might as well have forgotten about it. That's normal in a way. But Marco had managed. Serious. The reason was that he'd already retaken a million times and he was about the same age as Émilie Fermat. The proof? He gave her a kiss at the gate after school. It was the sort of thing that impressed most people. But me, it left me cold. Because I didn't give a toss about Émilie Fermat. The one I was more interested in was Mathilde, her younger sister, who was also in the fifth form and who I daren't speak to. When Mathilde Fermat looked you in the eye it made you shudder.

Marco had asked if I could come with him to the party. Émilie had agreed. "I managed to get you in", he'd told me, with the weary expression of someone who has just given you a free blood transfusion. He thought I was overjoyed to go to this girl's birthday party just because she was an actress and everything, while the truth was that if I was pleased it was most of all to be able see Mathilde. Because I thought she'd probably be there too. Since it was in their apartment after all. It would be a chance to talk. To see something of each other. They lived near the Champs-Elysées, and from what Marco had said there would be lots of actresses and everything. "Heaven on earth, if you like".

So I was disgusted not to be able to go in the end.

As a rule my mother would have rather seen me dead than let me go out during the week. I'm not joking. As it was, the weekend was always a drag. I'd have to sweet-talk her. But then, you might say that I couldn't quite see myself

explaining that I absolutely had to go to this party when the only excuse was that it was Émilie Fermat's birthday, the actress who shows her breasts, and that there'd be lots of others, actresses, really gorgeous I bet, who maybe bare their breasts too (seeing it's well-known that all actresses show their beasts sooner or later anyway).

Asking my mother that, as a rule, was a bit like bungee-jumping without the bungee. Suicide, pure and simple. But I'd managed to negotiate a possibility by telling her a ridiculous story. Okay, at first I thought of describing it to her as something worthwhile, like an evening in aid of world hunger. That was my mother's soft spot, world hunger. She loved it. Because of her religious side. But it wasn't convincing enough. She knew full well that world hunger wasn't exactly a passion of mine. I prefer tennis or literature. What worked out well, though, was that for once we didn't have school the next morning, which was a Saturday. They called it a staff training day. Fantastic. So as a result, Friday evening was part of the weekend. Just this once. Fine, but that wasn't necessarily enough with a mother like mine. The crafty thing I did was to tell her I'd got fantastic marks at the last staff meeting, which had been a few days before. *The perfect crime.* Seeing that was what interested my mother. Right. The truth was that I'd got crap marks, except in French. French, that's my best subject (as you're no doubt beginning to realise). Anyway. My mother was well excited. Because she suddenly got the impression I'd made progress and everything. So she said I could go to the party on Friday night. That knocked me dead.

I'd told everyone that I was going. I'd even dared to talk to Mathilde. She and I weren't in the same class, except for German. *Ich liebe dich.* We saw each other twice a week. All

27

through Tuesday's lesson that week I repeated the words to myself. Are you going to be at your sister's birthday party? At the end of the lesson I went for it, despite being scared stiff. "Yes," she said, with a little smile. And me, I almost had a heart attack.

But she went back on her decision, my mother. After a totally trivial bit of trivia. Marco and I had been caught smoking in the bogs between lessons. Three days before, what's more. Just bad luck, really. Nothing too serious, if you want my opinion. Except my mother took it ultra-badly. She always took unimportant things ultra-badly. She said I was going to turn into a delinquent. I'm not joking. That's what she said. When the bloke she lived with, François, he smoked more than a packet a day no problem. I know that because most of my fags were nicked from his study. Anyway. My mother wouldn't listen to a word on the subject. Not a word. For her, smoking was a crime. She was religious, I tell you. So things got heated. They even got overheated. Especially when she found out it was from François that I pinched my smokes. "He's the one who pays for your schooling, and this is how you thank him?" He was the one who called it a "fag end" instead of a "fag". How embarrassing, like. And he smoked with a cigarette holder. Like in the time of the pharaohs. In the Middle Ages. It was just to remind you he was an aristocrat, in case you hadn't noticed. Pathetic, that's what I think.

Where I was unlucky was that after the business with the fags, the Principal of the *Institute* had given me a warning, like it laid down in the school rules, and my mother had been called in to see him on the day of Émilie's party. I swear to you: that very same day. It set off a hyper-heated scene. There we were, the three of us, in the head's office. I won't describe the atmosphere. I got it with both barrels.

And afterwards, hopping mad, my mother refused to let me go out. If I thought I was going to Émilie Fermat's birthday party then I had another thing coming. I was in the wrong, I admit that. But I thought it was unfair, frankly. It's not right to go back on your word.

In retaliation I put up a poster in my room which I bought from a guy in the métro; it was of a man on a cross wearing a crown of thorns, and written underneath: '*He didn't smoke, he didn't drink, he didn't fuck: he died at the age of thirty-three*'.

3

WHEN YOU THINK about it, Marco was really lucky to be able to do what he liked. His parents must have been well decent to leave him on his own in Paris. They must have trusted him and everything. Decent people always trust you. That's how you recognize them. But even so I thought it was odd for parents to leave their son by himself in Paris without worrying or anything. "What are they doing abroad, your parents?" I asked, to shed some light on the mystery. He was barely listening to what I was saying. Too busy polishing his shoes for Émilie Fermat's party. He was the typical type of guy who didn't answer, Marco. You asked him a question: one time he'd answer, another time he wouldn't. You could never tell. It's always driven me nuts, that kind of attitude. Me, someone asks me a question, I answer. Question of logic. Him, no. He preferred cleaning his shoes so you were forced to notice they were making a statement, those shoes of his. "Not bad, eh?" He said it while he was looking in the mirror, as if it was himself he was talking to. I didn't answer. I wasn't about to answer him when he'd just been ignoring me. So I repeated: "And? Why aren't they in Paris, your parents?" He went into the bathroom, still ignoring me because I hadn't given him an answer. At the time it annoyed me. That's why I told him: "Stop poncing yourself up for a second. I asked you a question."

"Work. It's my father. He's in telecommunications."

"Where?"

"I've told you thousands of times … "

"I forgot."

"In Morocco."

This guy really had all the luck. His parents had left six months ago. Like they didn't want their son to go to a lycée, the international type of lycée, and they thought the *Institute* was an okay place, given its reputation, so they left him on his own in Paris. With a garret as a bonus. The first time he'd told me that it knocked me flat. Okay. Then later on I found out that that wasn't exactly how things were. It was just his version. The fact was his parents had left him with his grandmother, who lived on the ground floor of the building, but who also had a room in the attic. He'd managed to persuade her to let him sleep there. Mind you, the rest of the time he was supposed to live with the old girl. But of course he forgot to tell you that, Marco. He preferred you to think he lived alone. Like a student, like.

"I'd be really pleased if my parents went to Morocco, I would."

"What do they do, your parents?" he asked as he came back into the room.

He'd plastered his hair back. I don't know what he put on it to make it stay that way. I tried it once. Not to be the same as him, but because I liked it. It wouldn't hold. In the evening I came home with a sort of crest. Embarrassment. But with him it held. When he did it he looked like an Italian, the mafia type and everything. You could still see the traces of his comb.

"My father, it's complicated … "

I didn't want to dwell on the subject. I never talked about it, on account of him being dead.

"And your mother?"

"My mother, I'd rather not talk about her. She lives with this bloke … Fuck. He wears corduroy trousers."

"Oh, yeah. I know what you mean … "

"And the business with the warning, she just couldn't handle it. Sometimes I think the best thing would be to clear off."

"And where would you go?"

"Don't know. A long way away I think."

Marco gave me a funny look. I still hadn't told him that I wasn't going to be able to come to the party after all, but I got the feeling he'd guessed. The truth was I hadn't worked out how to explain without sounding like the type who gets told off by his mother. Sure, he'd been caught smoking: he must have had a warning the same as me, but no one could give a toss. Seeing there wasn't anyone there to give him grief (apart from his grandmother, who must have been fast asleep most of the time). But I had to take the plunge. So I told him straight out that I couldn't come after all. I had better things to do. An appointment. With a girl, ready and willing. So, obviously. I wasn't going to go to an actress's party when I'd got a date the same evening. I'd have to be stupid. And anyway, who the hell cared about actresses?

At first he didn't believe me. He thought I was just making it up. So I had to go into more detail. She was called Charlotte. A brunette from my last school who smoked at least a packet of cigarettes a day and who'd dyed her hair red. That's what convinced him, the bit about the red hair. It's not something you make up. That's my technique, me: give precise details right in the middle of an enormous lie. It avoids the question.

In any case, I didn't care if I was giving him a spiel. Because I knew he often did the same. Marco was the type to make up stories about himself day and night. Some incredible things happened to him, if you did but listen. Next to his life, yours was nothing but a washout. I know

people who'd have taken it all literally. But with him you could never take anything literally, seeing he made things up day and night. His problem was that he didn't have a great memory. In fact he had a totally crap memory. My theory was that he drank too much. So he came out with contradictory versions. If you want my opinion, the guy was always lying. Sometimes without even realizing. A kind of illness. Especially when it came to girls. He'd told me such incredible things that in the end I didn't believe a word. Even his story about Morocco was dodgy. That's why I kept bringing up the subject. He was the sort to tell me one day that his father worked in telecommunications in Tunisia. Or was it Maghreb? I'd have really loved to catch him in the act. Red-handed. So anyway, it didn't bother me if I shot him a line now and then. One good turn deserves another, in a way. Because obviously I didn't have a date with Charlotte. It was just because I couldn't come. On account of my mother.

"So why don't you bring her along?"

"Who?"

"The girl you've got a date with?"

"Which one's that?"

"The girl you've got a date with?"

"What?"

"The girl … "

"Which girl?"

"The one you've got a date with … "

"Which one?"

I was asking him this to gain time. Because I knew damn well which girl he was talking about: there weren't exactly a thousand girls I had a date with, seeing there was only one, and what's more I didn't have a date with her—but I wanted to confuse him a bit to give me time to come up

with a good excuse. What's annoying about people is that they're always pushing you to make something up. You'd really like to tell the truth, but they always see to it that they thwart you. No kidding, they always push you into inventing something. Because they never stop asking you to explain everything. Except it's not possible to explain everything all the time. For example, you tell them you can't go to a party and straight away they demand endless explanations, like a sick note, instead of just accepting that you won't be able to come. So you simplify a bit, you modify, you change things slightly so as not to go into detail, nothing really, a little face-lift, and then they accuse you of lying. That's what's annoying about people. Their lack of logic.

Why wasn't I bringing Charlotte to the party? I thought of telling him it was on account of money. Because maybe you had to pay to get in, mega-expensive sort of thing. Just to get in. And then there'd be drinks on top of that. In the end it would cost an arm and a leg. I've already told you, there were rich kids at the *Institute* who got more than a million in pocket money every week. I'm not joking. And in dollars, too … But that wasn't the case with me. So I couldn't go, and pay for two people, myself and Charlotte. I couldn't afford it. Because you might say I was broke right now. I'd spent everything I'd got.

Up till then it was thanks to Madame Morozvitch that I kept going. Denise Morozvitch. She at least was generous. She gave me a little allowance every week. In secret. Especially from her herself. Because she didn't really know about it. I didn't want to bother her with it. I thought it was better to take it from her discreetly. Out of politeness. But that scheme was finished with. That too, it had been

a pain. Actually, Madame Morozvitch lived in the same building as we did. The floor below. She was nice little old dear, but really very old. For example she was covered in bumps. You always got the impression she was going to die any minute. And first and foremost she was blind. Or almost. Anyway. My mother looked after her. She did her shopping for her, that sort of thing. The pair of them got on well. But then she liked that, my mother did, taking care of old women. It must have made her feel useful. Right. And since she thought I needed something useful to do with my life as well, she'd got me involved with her carry-on. By force, obviously. She'd decided that I had to drop in and see her once a week to take care of her. Horror. Well, it was a horror to start with. I didn't know what to say to her. I didn't even know if she'd worked out who I was, or what I was doing in her living room. She sat there in her armchair, motionless, with her big dark glasses, and me, like a twat, looking at her without knowing what to do. Anxiety. It went on for hours. Sometimes I said things to her, but she replied way off the point. Or she didn't even react. Because of her glasses you couldn't ever tell if she was asleep, or if she was just about to croak. So I behaved as if she was asleep. Basically, we got on better when we didn't speak. We didn't have anything more to say to each other.

But then I began to find the time dragged. Yeah. Two hours a week looking at those eyes behind her glasses, it could wreck your morale. I'm not joking. So I decided to read things to her. From the books that were on her shelves and which smelt of dust. I read them out loud. At the time I hadn't yet realised that I wanted to be a writer, seeing I knew nothing when it came to books. That was when we started to get on well, her and me. In fact she was a lot less dead than you expected. Sometimes she could come

out with things that bowled you over. About her life, for example. She had loads of stories to tell you. Incredible stuff. The rest of the time I read to her. And then one day she asked me to go and find a letter she had had. A letter in her writing desk. Because her son wrote to her from time to time. A real bastard, from what I could make out. Who thought of only one thing: putting her in an old folks' home so he could have her apartment. I swear to you. People like that still exist. There are more and more of them, even. Anyway. I went to look for the letter so I could read it to her. And it was while I was rummaging that I came across her hiding place. Where she kept her money. A wad, like in the films. I thought I was seeing things. At the time I didn't touch any of it. But I thought about it all that night. I told myself it was now or never. After all, she was blind. I wasn't taking any risks. The best thing, to my mind, was to nibble away at it gradually. So as not to be found out. Forewarned is forearmed. Maybe even well-armed, faced with a gaga old woman like Madame Morozvitch.

The following week I didn't think twice. I pretended to be just slipping out for a second, and I went into the next-door room again where what she called her 'writing desk' was, which was actually a table with drawers. I didn't waste any time. In fact I got a move on. I took two notes, both twenties. No one would be any the wiser. Not bad, eh! The easiest bank hold-up in the history of bank hold-ups! Great art. Signed Julien Parme. Then all of a sudden, as my hand hovered deliciously in the lovely drawer, I saw that Madame Morozvitch was standing by the door a few feet away, and that she was looking at me. Agh! I've never jumped so much in my life. There she was, tucked away behind her dark glasses, saying nothing. Suddenly I had my suspicions: what if she could see properly? I mean,

37

take an old woman who wears glasses: who tells you she's actually blind? She might just be wearing them so everyone *thinks* she's blind. Subtlety and all that. And so they act accordingly. I smiled awkwardly. Nervously, I shoved the two notes in my pocket. Now I had the feeling she was staring at me. I shut the drawer as quietly as possible. But she made a funny noise. With her mouth. As if she knew. It scared the hell out of me. Fuck. If my mother found out you might say I was done for. I suggested we go back to the living room. She gave a little witch's smile, a knowing smile, and then I settled her back into her armchair. I sat down as well, all innocent, I cleared my throat, because my voice always croaks slightly when I'm uptight, I don't know why, and I scratch my nose when I'm uptight too, it's the sort of thing I can't stop myself doing. So I cleared my throat while scratching my nose, and began to read.

She interrupted me right in the middle of a sentence: "You know, Julien, I wanted to say it's very kind of you to come and visit me like this."

I didn't know whether it was a hint or what. But I thought it was best to behave as if nothing had happened.

"Not at all, Madame Morozvitch. It's … normal."

My voice was getting completely out of control, and I'd soon look like Michael Jackson on account of scratching my nose.

"No, that's just the thing, it's not normal. That's why I'm so touched."

When I told you she sometimes came out with things that bowled you over …

"You have to try and be a bit generous," I put in.

Then as fast as I could I started reading again. She didn't say anything else that day. I took that as her consent. After all, it was better for her if I took it, the cash. Because if I

hadn't taken it it would have gone to her son. In the end, I mean. And since it was precisely that which interested him, her son, the cash, and that was why they didn't get on, mother and son, it was better for everyone if I took care of it, the cash. Simple question of logic. If I could do a good turn … Because deep down I liked her, Madame Morozvitch. Besides, one day I'd give back what I'd taken from her. I'd put the account straight. And I'd give it all back. I'd even give her a bit more, to cover the interest. And then I'd buy her some flowers. Now and again. With her money, obviously, but that's not what counts. What counts is that she thinks you're taking care of her. That you like her. That it smells nice in her room. Because it must be well depressing, if you want my opinion, to be as old as her. And blind into the bargain. I'd bring her flowers and cakes. That way, without realizing it, there'd at least be two of us who thought it was a good idea that I pinched a little from her every week.

That day, after an hour's reading, I felt ultra-rich. I had forty euros in my pocket. International class. What was more, I'd be able to do the same every week. A schoolboy, I was already dreaming of being a man of private means. I remember it well: I was like a madman, the weather was fine, it was the beginning of spring. It made me want to go and sit on the terrace of a café and laze in the sun. I went along to Alésia, a part of town where I didn't know anyone. When the waiter came over I said to him, with the voice of a writer at the height of his fame: "*Un whisky, please!*" For a moment he hesitated, given the time of day and also because of my age, I thought he was going to say no; but no, he didn't say anything, which means yes in waiters' language doesn't it? For his trouble, I told myself, I'll leave him a huge tip. I've always dreamt of leaving huge tips. To

see. The guy's face. In an instant he understood, the waiter, that he was dealing with Julien Parme. He couldn't believe his eyes. And I'd have hardly got up, been on the point of leaving, would have hardly gone a few yards, when you see him already running after me, Monsieur, Monsieur, all out of breath, sweating, all excited the guy, excited most of all, even overawed, the chance of a lifetime, he hands me a copy of my latest novel and asks if I would be so kind, do him the great honour, to sign the masterpiece for him … Yeah, I remember, I felt really rich that day, with forty euros in my pocket. Everything seemed possible to me, even becoming a great writer. I also remember that I bought a packet of cigarettes and smoked all afternoon in the sun, dreaming about all the novels I was going to be able to write. I felt great. No worries. With the incredible sensation of being free, having my whole life ahead of me.

Especially since for Madame Morozvitch it changed virtually nothing. What I mean is, it didn't matter to her. For me, on the other hand, it meant I could pay for smokes, movies, books and lots of other things too. And it was an extra incentive to come and see her every Saturday. At the end of the day, although I wasn't a thief, not at heart anyway, I didn't feel any shame, except for the constant, nagging one of not feeling any. Usually I lifted twenty euros. Rarely more. To begin with I kept a note of it all. Book-keeping for invalids. Then I stopped because I was always getting muddled up. I've never had a head for figures. But the day when I'd be able to pay it back, it would be easy to work out how much I owed her. Come to think of it, it would be a tidy sum. To be deducted from my royalties. So I'd have to talk to my publisher about it. Once I'd got one. Once I'd written a book.

Okay. But the problem was that one day her son packed her off to a nursing home. Although she was still perfectly well. But what he wanted was the apartment. Not that I'm bragging, but what proves me right about this was that he moved in a month later. Into her apartment. It made me want to puke. I'm sure he didn't even ask his mother what she thought about it, the son. That sort of thing, it makes you depressed for a month. Especially since I'd lost quite a lot of money over this business, seeing the writing desk was still pretty full. But I wasn't about to go and read to that moron just so I could carry on helping myself. That was out of the question. I don't make a habit of reading to morons. After all, I do have some principles.

4

MAYBE THAT'S WHAT I should have told Marco: I couldn't go because of money. It was a way of lying while telling the truth. But in the end I thought it was a bad idea: I could hardly see this girl making us pay to get in (I'm talking about Émilie Fermat). If it had been in a nightclub, okay, but at her place, I mean, and on her birthday, it wasn't likely, it sounded like an excuse, so I ought to have admitted the truth to him—ie: that because of my mother the 'night of the year' was going to pass me by. Yet all the same there was something disgusting about it.

So I wouldn't have to give Marco an answer right away, I lit a cigarette. That's what I like most about smoking: lighting up. It's what makes it, I think. Me, I always frown when I light a cigarette. For no particular reason. Some things can't be explained. You should explain that to people who think that everything can be explained. "Got one for me?" Marco was still looking at himself in the mirror. Stripped to the waist and everything. If he'd been able to kiss himself, this one, he'd have done it. I swear to you. It's crazy, but the guy was in love with himself. Well, good for him, if you want the truth. You had to admit that he had some success. You only had to see him and you knew immediately that he'd got what it takes with the girls. No doubt his age had a lot to do with it. And besides, he was a hunk. He put on a white shirt, really simple, look what style I've got sort of thing, then turned round to take the cigarette I was offering him and said for the fourth time:

"So why don't you bring her along then, the girl you've got a date with?"

"It's not her sort of thing, that kind of party," I replied eventually.

"Oh yeah? And what is her thing?"

He always had to have the last word. That gets on my nerves, people who always want the last word. Because there isn't a last word. Never. There's always another one, worming its way along just behind. That's basic knowledge. He should have known that, Marco. In the first place, how was I supposed to know what it was, her sort of party, Charlotte, seeing that me, I'd never met her, this Charlotte? He was getting me down with his endless preparations and millions of questions. I wanted to go home now. Fuck. Roll on the day when I was eighteen. Freedom. Because now, I felt a bit like a dog tied to a post. With a rope burning my neck. How many times had I heard it, that gaoler's expression: "When you're eighteen you can do what you like … "?

On the wall of my cell I was crossing off the days.

Marco turned to me. At last he was ready. "Well?" he asked. "You've forgotten your lipstick," I said. Just to show him I wasn't as strung out as I looked. "Don't worry," he replied, quick as lightning, "I'll have some soon enough, and not just on my lips … " That kind of hint irritated me. It's exactly what I was saying to you just now: nothing but show, pure and simple. Then he started telling me that he had to get a move on because he was expecting a girlfriend who was coming to pick him up before going on to the party. That didn't surprise me, the thing about the girlfriend who had to come and fetch him. In fact I'm sure he always did it. Much too much of a poser, this guy. It was to show he had a garret. He was giving her a preview of the décor, in a way. For after the party.

"So who is she, this girlfriend?"

"Wouldn't you like to know … "

"No … I don't give a toss."

I pretended to be looking for something in my pocket.

"She's called Charlotte too. Funny, eh?"

I wondered if he was taking the piss. Marco was exactly the sort of guy who'd say that to piss you off. No finesse, this bloke. I clicked my tongue. I don't know why I did it. Sometimes I do things without knowing why. Probably to show I wasn't rattled. Too bad if he didn't want to believe what I said about Charlotte. I wasn't about to beg him or anything. I got up from the chair. My legs were like jelly. "Right. I'm off." I was already late, but I didn't feel like going home, frankly: after what had happened in the head's office … He turned to me and said, with an odd smile:

"So who do you think it is, this girl?"

"I don't think."

"It's Mathilde."

I gulped.

"Who? Mathilde Fermat?"

"Yeah."

Fuck … It took me at least ten seconds to realise what he'd just come out with. What? Mathilde Fermat … Almost my fiancée … I could have collapsed on the spot … The worst news of the day. Of the year, even … At that moment his mobile rang. He went into the kitchen to answer it. So I couldn't hear, I imagine. Mathilde Fermat? I smacked myself on the forehead. I couldn't get over it. What the hell was she doing with a guy like Marco? Life is beyond comprehension. What did she see in him? A lumping great bloke like him. I didn't understand anything any more. He came back into the living room, which was also his bedroom. "Okay, this is all very well, but I'm going

to have to get a shift on. She's just coming." She'd called to let him know she was going to be slightly early. So now he was hyper. He started tidying up the gear that was scattered on his bed and armchair. This was all definitely moving too fast for me.

"I can't believe it … "

"What?"

"You told her I was here?"

"Told who?"

"Mathilde … "

"I don't know now. Fuck, see how you've gone and creased it for me! You're a real schmuck."

It's true I hadn't seen it, his shirt. But what a place to put it anyway, on an armchair. After all, a chair's for sitting in. So you shouldn't be surprised if a shirt that's been put on a chair ends up creased. Question of logic, pure and simple. But logic, Marco had never heard of it.

"How long before she gets here?"

"Right now. She said she was just coming. She wanted the code."

She was about to arrive. Fuck. She wanted the door code. I couldn't understand any more. I didn't know they knew each other, the two of them, seeing Marco didn't do German but Spanish. "Where do you know her from? Eh? I didn't know you knew each other … " I'd never seen them together or anything. And I'd never dared tell him, Marco, what I thought of her. I'd never dared tell him I thought about her every night before going to sleep, that she was probably the person I liked most in the whole world, with that mouth of hers, and that when I spoke to her the other day I nearly went out like a light. No kidding. Like a light. From emotion and everything. And now he tells me I'm going to see her here. No preparation. He was busy folding

46

his short-sleeved shirt as carefully as a girl does while I was maybe going to see Mathilde Fermat. Fuck. We weren't really on the same wavelength, him and me.

"And then you're going straight to the party?"

"Well, yeah."

"But why's she coming to your place when it's at her place?"

Now Marco was making his bed. And suddenly I thought that maybe he was going to bring her back here, the great pig. After the party. I don't know why, but the idea seemed horrible to me. The horror of horrors, even. I remembered what he'd said about the lipstick, too. The bastard. It was her he was talking about when he said he was going to have lipstick all over him. I wondered if Mathilde Fermat was the sort of girl who wore lipstick. Probably, when she went out for the evening. "But how come she's coming to your place?" He opened the window slightly to let in some fresh air. He inspected himself one last time in the mirror. Then he said. "You ready?" I rummaged in my pockets. A slight panic attack. I got a fag, which I lit with a frown. Except this time I knew why I was frowning. "This is crazy, fuck. And she's coming here?" "Any minute, I tell you." Maybe I'd meet her on the stairs. I had a rush of stress. I wondered if I'd be brave enough to speak to her. If I'd known I'd have worn my black jacket, the one I love. Because it's true, I hadn't been expecting this. It took me by surprise. I started to panic. Mathilde Fermat. And if she asked me why I wasn't coming to her sister's party? I'd have to stick around close to Marco. He was the type who'd just blurt out to her that my mother had punished me. A traitor, Marco. He wanted to put on some music. He was searching all over for a CD. I heard him muttering because he couldn't find the one he wanted. I asked him again, how

come and most of all why she was coming to his place and to do what. He remained vague. Because his mind was on his stereo. He wanted to get things in the mood. Fuck. Why wasn't I going to this party? I was disgusted. But most of all I wanted to be invisible.

"Right. I'm going then. You'll give her a kiss from me."

"No problem."

"And if she asks you why I'm not coming … "

"It'll be fine. Don't worry."

"Thanks. See you then."

"See you."

I walked out of the room. As I closed the door behind me I heard him say in his shit's voice: "And good luck with Charlotte!" Sometimes he really was a filthy creep. He was exactly the type to say good luck with Charlotte knowing full well you were going to spend the evening on your own. I pressed the lift button. It flashed in the darkness for ages. I wanted to get out of there. Because I was afraid I'd have nothing to say to her. And that she thought I was idiotic. I've never been so nervous. Mathilde Fermat. In the distance I could hear music. I told myself that Marco had found his CD. What a cunt, Marco. Then the lift arrived. And I went all the way down to the bottom in darkness, shivering like something does when it runs away.

5

WHEN I SAY: "I went all the way down to the bottom in darkness", I know that some people will try and be clever and tell me you can't say that. And I straightway reply that I'm aware of that. But what drives me nuts is individuals who correct you with a mocking expression when you use a stylistic device. For instance, if you say "I went down to the bottom", the character who replies ironically, asking you: "Oh right, so you didn't go down to the top then?" well nine times out of ten, that character, I want to kill them. I think that kind of little put-down is totally stupid, frankly. Because to my mind, when you say "go down to the bottom", you're saying it to be precise. And anyway, me, when I say that, if someone corrects me while quietly taking the piss, I straightway reply that you might very well go down to the top or up to the bottom, but it's very difficult to say because you need a poetic sense, and a poetic sense isn't given to everyone, especially not morons who think they speak better French than other people.

I walked home, and all the way I didn't see anything that was going on around me, I was thinking about her so much. I went into the entrance of my building. Generally speaking, I never take the lift up. Question of principle. Lifts, they're for old people and Eskimos. That's why, generally speaking, I always use the stairs. And also, generally speaking, I run up. Firstly because I'm always pushed for time. Like all great writers. But mostly I do it out of instinct. It's my legs, they go mad the moment I'm

on the first step. Don't ask me why, I've no idea. It's just that when I see stairs, I start running. I can't help it. So as usual I was out of breath when I got to the door of the apartment. On the top floor. More than anything I wanted to throw up. Everything made me want to throw up, if you want the details. The floors I'd just come up. The false marble of the staircase. The door in front of me. What was on the other side of it. I mean my mother and everything. Total disgust. I imagined turning round and leaving. I don't know where. Just leaving. Telling them all to go to hell. And then going to the party, seeing Mathilde again. Telling her I love her. Living, like. If life was a novel, I thought, that's what I'd do. That's what I'd do if I had the courage. Life is a novel when you've got the courage. Fuck. An aphorism. Oh my God! Sometimes I was capable of coming out with phrases like that! Quickly I got a pencil from my bag, I sat on the top step and made a note of it somewhere so as not to forget it. Then I circled it twice. And I wrote next to it: '*For the novel*'. Phrases like that, I'm not bragging, but I've got them pretty much everywhere among my stuff. The day I write them up they'll make a real novel. I swear to you. On the first page you'll see: '*For Mathilde, who inspired me*'.

I sat on the top step for quite a while. The light had gone out by itself. And I let my mind wander in the darkness, not moving. I also wanted a cigarette, but that was a bit risky. On my own doorstep. Seeing I'd got my mother believing I was going to stop. But the craving was too strong, so I went and opened the little skylight a few steps further down, and lit a cigarette, frowning. Like in the films. Yeah, leave. That would be classy. Go to Italy, for example. Italy, I'd seen photos, it was the most beautiful country in the world. The land of tiramisu. I'd be able to fend for myself there,

definitely. I'd work to earn a bit of cash, just so I could live in a little hotel by the sea, and it would be the good life. In the evening I'd go to bars to chat up girls. I'd talk about my adventures. Okay, I'd exaggerate slightly about my reasons for leaving. But not too much. Just the odd murder here and there. Just to make the whole thing more sexy. And they'd fall in love with me. And then I'd write a letter to the *Institute*. I can see the look on all their faces already. Sick, those guys. And another letter to Madame Thomas, explaining why, despite our shared passion for literature, I couldn't ask her to join me; I was soon going to marry Mathilde.

I gave a deep sigh. I heard the telephone ring on the other side of the door. And my mother's voice. It must have been at least nine o'clock. I was going to get a mouthful—fact. Especially as I hadn't got an excuse or anything. But oddly enough I took my time. I had a mint tic tac for my breath. I told myself that at this very moment, Mathilde must be in that bastard Marco's room. I could just imagine him getting her a drink. Wine, the whole great game. Or worse: a Coke with an aspirin in it. I'd heard that that drove girls completely wild when it came to sex. An aphro-dickiac, like. Frankly it made me sick.

I opened the skylight again to throw out my cigarette butt. You always have to dispose of the evidence. Going into the apartment with a cigarette butt in your pocket would be a bit like killing a bloke and still having the gun on you when you went through customs. I'm not totally mad. I leant out so I could make sure it fell, the butt. I watched it for as long as possible. It suddenly vanished, as if by magic. A disappearance. I imagined a body falling. I imagined it was me, the body. It sent a shiver down my spine. I closed the skylight and thought of something else.

I went back up to my floor. I got my key and, just as I was going to put it in the lock, the door opened. It was Bénédicte, she had probably heard me. In my opinion she'd been lying in wait for me. At any rate, that was the sort of thing she'd do.

"Oh, there you are … we've been looking for you everywhere. You're going to get a roasting, my lad. I wouldn't want to be in your shoes … "

She said it as if butter wouldn't melt in her mouth. It made me hyper-annoyed. For a moment I didn't move, like I was paralysed, because I could hear a voice inside me saying: "Leave! Go as far away as possible! Split! You haven't got any well-wishers in this dump! Leave while there's still time … have courage!" I looked out of the skylight. Outside it was dark. It was late. I took a deep breath to calm myself, there'd still be time to clear off later, and I went into the apartment. Like a good boy.

I realise I haven't told you about Bénédicte yet. She's François's daughter, him with the 'de'. A kind of stepsister if you like. But what's strange is that she looks really like my mother. Facially, I mean. Although they're nothing to do with each other, biologically speaking. Everyone says they look as if my mother were actually her mother. Which isn't the case, seeing she's mine, my mother. Whenever someone told them that they looked happy, the pair of them, as if they took it for a compliment, when most of the time it was just a passing comment. And François, it really pleased him too, the idea that his wife and his daughter looked similar. It was only me who was left completely cold by it. As long as no one told me I looked like François …

Him and my mother started living together almost two years ago. I was still a teenager then. I must have been about twelve, going on thirteen. One day we changed apartment and moved in here with them. Before, with my mother, we lived in quite a small place. But I liked it. While here it's an ultra-big apartment with a view of the Eiffel Tower. No kidding. Near the Trocadéro. That's when I met Bénédicte. To start with I thought she was quite pretty. She had long blond hair, very straight, which came nearly all the way down her back. But we never really got on, her and me. In fact we did nothing but quarrel. She was two years older than me. Marco's age. They met once, the pair of them. He came round to get something, we were in my room and she walked in without knocking as usual. Later, Marco talked to me about her, Bénédicte. He thought she was gorgeous and everything. According to him she had seriously nice tits. Maybe. But she was a real bitch. For example, she went riding every weekend. Girls who are mad about horses are always uptight and hard to get on with. That's a rule. Take a girl who goes riding every week, and well, she'll be mega-immature about life. The type who says she's not interested in boys. A permanent little girl always ready to lecture people. A quibbler. Forever saying her prayers, tidying up or getting on with her work. No, girls like that, frankly they're everything I can't stand. Especially since usually, that sort of girl, they can't stand boys like me. Poets, I mean.

The truth is she was bored with her life. But she was too proud to admit it. She would never have dared say something like that. For example, she was always in her room, working. And if you asked her why she hadn't finished, seeing she'd been working for hours by then, she told you she was getting ahead. Getting ahead, that means

doing exercises that aren't for the next day, but for the next few days. Bénédicte was exactly the sort of girl to get ahead. So obviously, she was bored. That's the kind of idea that people who are bored have, getting ahead. And when you're bored, you're the type who spies on other people's lives, the ones who've got a life, the type who waits by the door so the moment they come in you're the first to jump on them and tell them in your butter-won't-melt-in-my-mouth voice: "You're going to get a roasting, my lad. I wouldn't want to be in your shoes … "

So that's what I mean.

I made straight for my room to dump my things. Dinner was usually in the kitchen. At the other end of the apartment, that is. I went to the bathroom to give my face a quick wash. And to clean my teeth. You can never be quite sure with tic tacs. And faced with my mother, it's best to have cast iron defences. Given the situation, I ought to have got a move on to join them. But that day, I don't know why, I wasn't afraid how my mother would react. It was different. I took my time. I was too disgusted over the business with Mathilde. Nothing else mattered. You could have yelled at me as much as you liked. Suddenly I had an idea: to ring Marco's grandmother and tell her I was with him in his garret, that she absolutely had to come and see him right away because he wasn't feeling well and he'd been sick everywhere. Of course, he'd have told Mathilde that he lived on his own, like a student, and that his parents were abroad—just to show off—and in the middle of his performance, his grandmother would turn up with suppositories to settle his bowels. It really appealed to me, that idea. Uh-oh! But I heard reproving footsteps coming

down the corridor. And I went back to my room pronto without having time to put my plan into action.

My mother walked in right behind me. "So this is the time you come home?" She gave me a really hard look. It was harder than stone. Like her heart. I always had the feeling she didn't really love me, my mother. I think she'd got herself a very definite idea of what it was, a son, and I was the opposite of that idea. The one she'd have liked as a son, I could see him very clearly. I only had to close my eyes and he stood in front of me. He looked down on me from above, with an ironic, mocking smile, which meant: "You'll never make it, my lad ... It's me she loves". He was blond, like her. He was a good pupil, cultured, with well-turned phrases. He wanted to be an engineer, and he'd be really keen on scale models, for example. For his birthday every year my mother would buy him a new model. It wasn't difficult. You always knew what to get him, and every time he was mega-pleased, and he never stopped saying thank you. Whereas me, the look on my face last year when she gave me some thing that came in different pieces that you had to stick together and paint to make this really weird plane. Fantastic present. I told her I wasn't ten years old now, and that a scale model, it wasn't exactly what a man dreamed of. But that was what she refused to accept, that I wasn't a child any more. While the other one, the blond, he always said thank you. And he skipped a class nearly every year, since he got ahead so much in the evening, after school, instead of hanging out with his mates like I did, and smoking into the bargain. At staff meetings he always came away 'highly commended'. The perfect type, like. I could see it all in her eyes. And it froze me out.

"I'm talking to you. So this is the time you come home?" I said "Yes." She seemed outraged by my reply. As if I

was provoking her. Me, if you ask me a question, I reply. That's all. After all, I wasn't going to say "no", since she knew full well that that was the time I'd got back. What an idea, asking questions you know the answer to and which you know will annoy you. Only a mother would do that. Have I already told you that all mothers are losers? I could see things might get worse. So I tried to find an excuse, sharpish. Why did I get back so late? I took a quick look at the clock above my desk. It was gone half-past eight. That would be hard to talk my way out of. Seeing school finished about six. But I could always shoot her an enormous line. At that moment I saw Bénédicte's face appear round the door. She didn't want to miss any of the roasting, miss holier-than-thou. She was the perfect scale model of a stepdaughter. My mother adored her. And above all, she adored adoring her. It was a real reconstituted family, with people really loving each other. I was the only blot. In fact, the one single problem in their lives was me.

At the time I told myself it was true, they were terribly alike these two. What they were both missing was a heart. And once that occurred to me, I'd had enough of it. Yeah, right that minute. Just like that. I spoke my mind. I said: "I know. It's late. So what? I was with Marco. We were talking. I didn't notice the time. It's not exactly a big deal!" My mother didn't like you talking to her like that. She was the one who decided what was a big deal. Her, not you. Especially in the crappy situation I was in now.

"What do you mean, it's not a big deal? Two hours I've been waiting for you, Julien!" my mother replied, livid. "It's almost nine o'clock. That's no time to be coming home! Do you hear? And the same week you got a warning on top of that!"

I shrugged because I didn't know what to say. She had a despairing look, as if I was pushing her to the limit simply by existing. "What have I done to have a son like this? What have I done, eh?" That, that was typical of what she said whenever she wanted to let me know that she couldn't put up with me any more. She said it without looking at me, up at the ceiling, that's to say towards God who was just the other side, according to her. On the seventh floor. But God didn't give her an answer. He left her all alone with her pathetic question. What had she done to have a son like me? If she thought back a bit, she certainly ought to remember what she'd done to have me. Seeing there aren't exactly a thousand ways to have a son. Me, anyway, I had my own ideas about it, and the angrier she got, the harder I found it to imagine that she could have been that woman, sweet, young, in bed with my father, like two lovers, Mathilde and me for example, doing dirty things. Except that at the moment, the sort of thing she'd done to have me, it was that bastard Marco who'd be making the most of it with Mathilde instead, and that, it drove me nuts. My mother was bollocking me but I couldn't give a damn. My heart was elsewhere. Everything she said just ran off me. That's all I had in my mind: the fact that Marco must be busy chatting up Mathilde. With hints about tonight and everything. At the time it really made me ultra-annoyed. She was just yelling, and that was when I got onto dodgy ground.

"Why are you always shouting?" I asked.

"I beg your pardon?"

"You enjoy it, that's what it is, yelling all the time ... I don't know, can't you speak calmly?"

"Don't talk to me like that, Julien. Stop talking like that right now!"

"But it's you who never stops yelling! And if you want my opinion, that's not very smart. Yeah. It's not very smart talking to me like that. Because I'll remind you that in a few years time, it'll be me who decides which old people's home you go into … "

She changed colour right before my eyes. I knew I'd gone too far. But that night I was really desperate. It's true. I wasn't in control any more. I couldn't stop myself. Suddenly, François's cancerous voice could be heard calling my mother. It was like the bell in the middle of a boxing match. It was time. Time for what? Then I realised she was wearing an evening dress and everything. They were probably going out for dinner or something.

"Are you making fun of me? How dare you talk to me like that? Eh? Do you actually realise the situation you're in?

"Catherine!"

It was the handle's voice again. He was always stressing out about being late. My mother paused for a second before replying: "Okay. You're in luck, I haven't got time now. I've got to go. But we'll talk about it tomorrow. Believe you me, Julien, the two of us are going to have a little talk. We've got a lot to say to each other. See you tomorrow." She turned on her heel. You'd have thought we were in a bad film. With a bad actress who's trying to make you think that just at that moment she's supposed to be mega-angry. But then, before going out the door, she stopped dead. Sort of thunderstruck. She looked at me as if she was about to say something important, even really important, she opened her mouth, but in the end she didn't say anything. Strange. After which she left the room, followed immediately by Bénédicte. "Good riddance" I said once they were at the end of the corridor and couldn't hear. Women, it's simple:

either you love them or you hate them. In their case, the two of them, it didn't take long to decide.

I heard the front door slam. It echoed in my head like an interlude. I took a deep breath. I lay on the bed. What had I done to have a mother like that? That was the real question. Because frankly, my crime was hardly going to kill anyone. The only explanation for all this was that I was in love. That's all. But she couldn't understand that, my mother. Seeing she hasn't got a heart and that 'being in love' will never mean anything to her, my mother. Not since the death of my father.

I closed my eyes and thought about him, telling myself that things wouldn't have been like this if he hadn't have left us in the lurch. It's true. Then I started talking to him, like I often do. I know it's stupid, talking to someone who's dead. But I've always done it, me. Bénédicte often takes the piss out of me because she thinks I'm talking to myself. She says I'm mad. But try explaining to her that it's my father I'm talking to, and that it's the only way I can find of not being really unhappy. Try explaining that to a girl who goes riding every week …

6

BÉNÉDICTE WAS RUMMAGING around in her room. I could hear her through the wall, moving about. I sensed she was lying in wait. What for? The chance to come and bug me, no doubt. It's a shame, because I'd have loved to have a mega-friendly sister, me, one you could talk to about everything. But her, she was so all-over frustrated that you couldn't talk to her about anything. Or just about horses. But me, I didn't want that. Question of principle. Especially since I knew her tune off by heart. Every Saturday she went to her club. On the outskirts of Paris. Near a forest. I can't remember which one now. Sometimes she went in for competitions. At first I used to go and watch her. She made me laugh, with her riding hat and her crop. If I'd ridden horses, I'd have rather worn another kind of outfit, me. Because a hard hat and a crop, that's really the pits. The only way to ride a horse, to my mind, is like in the films. With a proper hat. If not, it's really the pits. A bit like skiing in a balaclava. The sort of thing wallies do, if you see what I mean. I imagined myself arriving at the lycée with the horse, the hat, the business. Lifting Mathilde into the saddle. Telling her that maybe we weren't going to spend our whole lives in this miserable place. That it was time to go. Far away. Far, far away. To the other side of the desert. My horse would rear up, and away to adventure! Yeah. And Marco would watch us disappear over the horizon like a twat …

Bénédicte was about seventeen. I imagined asking her to come with me to Émilie Fermat's party. Without telling

our parents. That would give her a shock, little Miss Self-Righteous. But it wasn't really a serious idea. Because even if one day I did ask her, Bénédicte, to come to a party with me, she'd refuse outright. Just on principle. The principle being that anything to do with me disgusts her. No kidding. She often says that. All because we use the same bathroom and she thinks I take years to have a shower. (It's not my fault if I'm clean.) And also because I once tried to drown her cat. That caused a real scene. It was called Puss. I'm not joking. That on its own tells you a lot about the girl. Calling her cat Puss. Only a girl who's totally dippy would call her cat that. A girl who's right in the head would call it something else. But Puss, that's really for the crazies. I never got on with that cat, me. Always getting under my feet, spying on what I was doing, leaving tons of fur on my bed. A pain of a cat, basically. But, *what a coincidence*, it was Bénédicte's best friend. It purred whenever she came near. They were always cuddling each other all over the place. With an animal I think that's gross, me. Then one day I tried a little experiment. I'd run a bath. (As a rule I'd rather take a shower. But that day, don't ask me why, I'd run a bath.) Puss was prowling around in the vicinity. And since Bénédicte had ratted on me to our parents because she said I'd stolen some money that was on the chest of drawers, I'd decided to get my own back. Especially since my mother had been mega-strict. She'd shouted at me before even asking herself if it was really me. Amazing! No such thing as innocent till proved guilty in this dump! Under those conditions, me, I'd have rather given the money back right away. You might say all hell broke loose. So basically she deserved a small, symbolic punishment. That's how I got the idea of running a bath and throwing Puss in.

After some Olympic efforts he managed to get out of the bathtub. He didn't look quite so full of himself. He even slunk up against the wall, now he was soaking wet. It gave me a good laugh, frankly. Then, to be kind, I'd wanted to pretty him up again with the hairdryer, but he'd put on his airs and graces so I let him be. Bénédicte went wild with rage when she found out what I'd done. Two days later he died. Heart attack and everything. I swear to you. All of a sudden: he was there, he lay down and pop, he snuffed it. I honestly think it had nothing to do with the bath I'd given him. But Bénédicte, she was convinced of it. As far as she was concerned I'd deliberately traumatized him into having a heart attack. She treated me like a murderer. From that moment on she hated me. Although the vet told her it wasn't my fault. He had had a heart murmur, that cat. But she was having none of it. In her room, next to all her posters of horses, she put up a framed photo of Puss. At night, before going to sleep, she meditated in front of it. No kidding.

I opened the door to my room again. Not a sound in the whole apartment. The way was clear. I went to the kitchen to make some dinner. When our parents were out, I usually got myself something on a tray which I ate in my room. Or in front of the TV. The risk with the TV was that Bénédicte turned up every three minutes to criticise the programme you were watching and to ruin your life. So I preferred my room. Before opening the fridge I automatically switched on the radio in the kitchen. For a moment I flicked through the channels until I found some really beautiful music, only sad as hell. I carried on listening without knowing what it was. It killed me. I had tears in my eyes. I couldn't

understand the words because it was in disjointed English,
but I was sure it was talking about what was in my heart.
After the shitty day I'd had. As a result, what I longed for
was a cigarette. To be far away, smoking a cigarette. There's
something, I don't know whether you've noticed, but
sadness always makes you long to be far away and smoking
a cigarette. And besides, when you're also a writer, it makes
you crave a cigarette. When the music finished I got a bit
of paper that was lying around, and a pencil. I closed my
eyes (my technique for finding inspiration). What could I
write? At first I thought of a poem. A poem for Mathilde,
for example. That was a good idea. I opened my eyes to
make a start. But nothing came. I wasn't concentrating.
And I was all hunched up over the breakfast bar. So I sat
down. I put the sheet of paper in front of me, right in front,
I cleared my throat and I closed my eyes again. Maximum
concentration. I tried to imagine some powerful images.
For example, Mathilde. I was already choked up, just at
the idea that I was going to write my first real poem that
would go down in history. Something really impressive,
with rhymes. I opened my eyes again. The inspiration
would come, that was for definite. But I was thirsty. I got
up and had a drink from the tap. I looked out the kitchen
window. It faced onto the courtyard. Sometimes, if you
leant out, you could see into the apartment opposite.
I always got the feeling that I'd catch a naked woman
walking past the window. I went and sat down and I stayed
in front of the sheet of paper for a long while, thinking
about the publication of my collection of poems. I could
see myself on the back cover already, a black and white
photo, smoking a cigarette sort of thing, eyes mad with
despair. Or a cigar, I don't know yet. I'd send it to Madame
Thomas, this collection. And to all the girls who'd ignored

me. They'd kick themselves, the slags: they'd let slip the one and only opportunity to be the everyday inspiration of one of the century's greatest writers. Too bad for them. It was too late. They'd beg me to come back, but I'd remain impassive, despite the physical hints they made. I tore up the blank sheet in front of me and found another one. I got up to have a drink from the tap again before coming back to sit down. I was ready. To work! But nothing came. So I applied the good old technique of closing my eyes. Clenching my teeth this time. To force the ideas to come. Then I opened them again. Still nothing. Strange. This wasn't a good place to write. A kitchen, it's never produced any masterpieces. That's well known. So I opened a few cupboards. I got a tin of cake. My dinner. As well as one of the bottles of wine that were lying around. All the great writers are alcoholics. That's well known too. I slipped one under my shirt in case I bumped into Bénédicte. I got the corkscrew from the drawer and shoved it in my pocket. No need for a glass, I'd drink it from the bottle. Like Balzac and the others. Then I went out of the kitchen. After all, it was the ideal evening to begin it, my great novel. Yeah, all things considered, a novel, that was more suitable than a poem. I'd tell it all: the party I couldn't go to, the solitude in my room, the view of the Eiffel Tower lit up from the living room, my mother in the head's office, wanting to cry in Mathilde's hair—everything that was on my mind. A classic, like. I tiptoed through the apartment. I'd almost got to my room when I heard Bénédicte behind me: "What are you doing?"

I stiffened.

"What?"

"What are you doing?"

"Nothing. None of your business."

"You think I didn't see you?"

"If you mean the bottle I've got under my shirt, I don't really see what you're talking about."

She didn't say a word. It gave me time to get to my room and lock the door behind me. There was no way you could get any peace to write novels in this dump! I put all my writing materials on the desk and opened the window. I began by wondering what the title of the book would be. Personally, I think a great novel ought to have a great title. Because a great novel with a small title, that looks like narrowness and false humility. And a small novel with a big title sounds really pretentious: the "I'm the only one who hasn't noticed that I write bird droppings" sort of thing. Another solution is to write a small novel with a small title, but then you might as well stay at home. No. There's only one solution for writers like me, the great ones I mean, and that's a killer of a title. Something like *Journey to the end of the night*, but I'd looked it up, it's already taken. Suddenly someone knocked on my door. It was Bénédicte. That's why I said:

"Who's that?"

"Who do you think?"

"What do you want?"

"I've got to talk to you."

I hesitated for a moment.

"I'm working."

"At what?"

"I'm getting ahead."

She obviously didn't believe me.

"Listen … "

"What now?"

"Open the door."

"Someone with a name like Bénédicte ought to keep her trap shut," I replied.

It's true as well, fancy being called Bénédicte.

"If you were in my place … "

"If I was in your place, frankly I'd be long gone by now."

Thwack! Good shot. Right between the shoulder blades! This time she didn't have an answer. In fact she didn't make a sound for quite a while, but I knew she was still outside the door. I ignored her. I wondered what she'd done with her life before she met me. What did she do with her time? Who did she take it out on? And now, because of her and her presence under the door, I'd lost the thread of my thoughts. Oh yes: the title. To get some inspiration I took the corkscrew from my pocket. Then Bénédicte went on:

"That bottle you took, no way should you open it!"

"Which bottle?"

At that moment there was the sound of a cork coming out.

"It's for our parents, Julien. They've got to try it first. What are you doing? Wait! It's for the wedding. Do you hear me?"

I almost choked in the middle of a colossal mouthful. I even spilt some on the carpet. Which wedding? I opened the door. Her face was like something from a bad dream.

"Which wedding?"

"Which do you think?"

And she shot back to her room. Fuck. She was really pathetic from going riding every Saturday. I followed her to her room. Bénédicte! I'd risen to the bait. But I still wanted to know. She tried to shut the door but I wedged my foot in it. I didn't have any trouble opening it, since obviously I'm stronger than her. She was smiling all over her face. Shining with perversity. She disgusted me.

"What are you talking about?"

"Nothing."

She really did take me for an idiot. I grabbed her and started choking her. I squeezed my fingers round her throat as hard as I could. She began to scream. She made funny noises. You'd have thought it was a cow having its throat cut. Or an old hag, more like. It was more high-pitched. Then I let her go. "You're a real loser! A sad case! You're just like your father! Completely sick! You ought to be locked up! That's what they should do! Lock you up like your father!"

Here we go again. The same old tune.

"Whose wedding, Bénédicte?"

"Get lost."

"Tell me or I'll do it again!"

I went up to her intending to wring her neck. In return she gave me a smack round the face. Whack. A real cracker that rang out round the room. It was then I realised what she meant. Suddenly I could hardly breathe. I swear to you. I felt ill. I sat on her bed. My eyes were stinging. Even burning. Bénédicte was frightened. She sat next to me and asked me umpteen times if I was alright. She must have felt guilty for clouting me. Then she tried to cheer me up. But I didn't move. She flapped around me, like she was in a panic. She was talking non-stop. A lunatic. But I wasn't really listening to the double talk she was giving me, like how she'd put her foot in it, that's why she'd flown off the handle, she was annoyed with herself, she'd forgotten— so she said—that I didn't know about it yet, about the wedding business, it had just slipped out because of the bottle of wine …

"Liar," I replied eventually. "You knew full well I didn't know. In fact that's why you told me. Out of spite."

"It wasn't. I'd forgotten."

68

"I know full well you knew."

"That I knew what?"

"That I didn't know."

"I promise you I didn't … "

"And since when have you known about their wedding?"

"I don't know … Two or three days. If that. I walked in while they were talking about it. So then they told me … they were probably going to tell you too."

"So why haven't they told me yet?"

"They were going to tell you, I'm telling you. But seeing you're … mega-unpredictable and touchy … I expect they wanted to do it at the right moment."

The right moment. Fuck. What a bunch of traitors! My mother must have very likely been dreading telling me because she knew I couldn't stand him, François. The big-time turd. That was probably why she'd been more pleasant recently. Why she agreed at first that I could go to Émilie Fermat's party, for instance. Yeah, I suddenly realised she'd been preparing the ground for at least ten days. Before I got caught having a drag between lessons. I was nauseated.

I stood up. "Where are you going?" I had tears in my eyes now. I definitely didn't want Bénédicte seeing me like that. It would have made a great to-do if I'd bawled like a girl in front of her. Especially as it wasn't out of sadness that I had tears in my eyes. It was just my eyes, they were stinging from the tears. "Leave me alone," I replied. And I went back to my room and slammed the door behind me: that was the clout I'd have liked to give her in return.

I was feeling something indescribable. Not just sadness, not only that, but alarm or something. It was odd, but I'd never imagined my mother would get married again one

day. For me, marriage, it needed to be tied in with love and wanting children. Did they love each other? I'd never believed their stories about romance, me. To me it was more of an arrangement between them. The proof was they slept in separate beds in their room. Suddenly I wondered if they did it. Up till then, I know it's pathetic, but I'd never asked myself that. And now all of a sudden, because of the word 'wedding', unbearable images flashed through my mind: my mother naked on a bed, François on top of her, going at it, their two bodies, their little cries and their breathing mingling like in the films. It was repulsive. And I thought about my father, all alone. That night, that dreadful night when it all started, as I was weighing up the consequences of the word 'wedding', I couldn't help but think of my father. Yes, all alone, down there. What would he think about this? Wouldn't he be saying to himself that we were making a fine new life for ourselves? I mean: without him, in the warm, and in a lovely apartment in the Sixteenth into the bargain? If I were him, all this would have really made me sick. And anyway, I couldn't go along with it. That would be to betray my father. Suddenly I realised she was going to take his 'de'. She was going to change her name. Catherine de Courtois. Fuck. It was awful. And me, was I going to have to change my name too? Julien de Courtois? Never. It's not possible for a novelist to change his name. Then readers wouldn't know who he was any more. Me, I was Julien Parme. End of story. Like my father.

Ever since we'd lived in this apartment I sensed my mother couldn't bear me any longer. And now I discovered she wanted to marry that waster. I really couldn't understand why. More than anything I got the feeling it was bad for

me, and that it wouldn't be long before they wanted to get rid of me, seeing that François and me, we didn't get on at all, there were always arguments, and that by marrying him she was bound to take his side. She might as well have abandoned me on the side of the road, it would have been much the same.

I got up and went into their bedroom. Looking for a clue. I saw it differently now, this room. What was strange was that it was actually at a wedding that they'd met, the pair of them. And look where that had got us. Into the shit. With Bénédicte as a free gift.

On the piano there was a photo of François. I had a good look at it. He looked liked a retard. With his little scarf round his neck. Even when it's not cold. For me it was obvious, my mother couldn't love this bloke. Next to my father there was no comparison, not for a second. You just had to look at the photos, it stuck out a mile. The only thing he'd got going for him, François, was his money. But of course my mother, she'd always loved that, nice apartments and everything that goes with it. It made me think of what Marco had told me one day, as regards women. According to him there was only one thing that interested them, and that was money. What proved it, he'd said, was that ugly guys with loads of money all went out with babes. That was why he wanted to go to business school after the *bac*, Marco.

I went through some of their things but I didn't find anything of much interest. I sat at the piano. I tried to play a little tune, after my fashion. But I soon stopped. I'm hopeless when it comes to music. Then I sat where my mother does her makeup. I didn't know what I was doing, or what I was looking for exactly, but I started putting on lipstick. Like people in the circus. I was just messing

around. Stuck in the frame of the mirror was a photo of my mother. In it she was beautiful. I compared it with myself in the mirror. To see if we were really alike, her and me, now I had girl's lips. I dragged my hair back like she did. I don't know why, but that photo, looking at it too much made me feel melancholy. In it my mother looked like how I used to see her when I was small. I trusted her totally back then. Well, things had really changed.

I went into their bathroom and threw the lipstick down the bog. The whole tube. For no particular reason. And I tore the photo into little pieces. I was a bit worked up, like. I wanted to get my own back on something, without really knowing what. I said to myself: "If they get married, I'm out of here". I felt like an orphan. That's it: like an orphan. Betrayed by my mother. Then I flushed the toilet. I don't know why I did it, but watching the swirls of red in the bowl I got the feeling of achieving something significant. Yeah, things had really changed. Now I knew who she was, my mother. I'd seen her real face. I couldn't lie to myself about it any more. I wasn't a child any longer.

7

A BIT LATER in the evening I heard the front door slam. They were back from dinner. I'd been in my room for quite some time. Lying on my bed. Sorting things out in my head. What time was it? I didn't want to switch the light on so as not to attract attention. Midnight, perhaps. I waited a while longer. Eventually I began to feel rather hungry. But I thought it best not to leave my room. In case. I waited till all the lights were out then got up. I was still dressed. I felt like a burglar. I frightened myself. Because what scares the hell out of me more than anything is the idea of coming face to face with a burglar. Apparently it happens. I'm not joking. I tiptoed to the kitchen. I opened the fridge as if it was a safe. But there was nothing in it that I really fancied. I just poured a glass of milk. After I'd had a mouthful I noticed I'd left red marks on the rim of the glass. I'd forgotten to take off the lipstick. What a jerk. I looked at my face reflected in the shiny metal door of the fridge. A sad clown. I said to myself that at that moment, Mathilde and the others must already be enjoying themselves. They were probably drinking coloured cocktails and everything. While here I was with my glass of milk, looking at my reflection in a fridge door. I took a deep breath. Life is unfair. I don't know why, but it made me think of the deceitful light from dead stars. Then I headed back to my room, dragging myself along like a man condemned to death although no one knows he's actually innocent.

I didn't feel like sleeping. And if there's anything I can't stand, it's getting into bed when I don't feel like sleeping. Because I toss and turn and ideas rear up like spooked horses, which then means I want to sleep even less than before. Sometimes I stay awake till the early hours. I swear to you. And the feeling I had was that that was what was going to happen. So I stayed in the living room doing nothing. Sitting on the sofa, waiting for the lights to go out on the Eiffel Tower. A pointless display. Like the stars in the sky. I thought about everything all over again. It was the worst day of my life, come to think of it. Then I got up. I was looking for something to do. I remembered that to start with, during the first few weeks after moving to this apartment with my mother, I'd gone to see Bénédicte a few times while she was asleep. She usually slept in a little pair of knickers and a T-shirt. She was really beautiful like that. I stayed in the darkness, just a few inches away from her, watching her. It sent shivers right through me.

Once I went into the bathroom when she was taking a shower. She screamed. Although it was her who'd forgotten to lock the door. Serious. I'd seen her stark naked. How many times had I thought about it since, that image that lasted a fraction of a second? Thousands, at least. I tried to drive all these ideas from my mind. But I couldn't. So I shut my eyes and tried to imagine Mathilde in the shower. It was like playing with fire. Me, I've always had the impression that it's really dangerous to dream too much. It gives you false hopes. And hope, that's what kills you. Even if most people would have you believe it's that that keeps them alive.

I walked out of the living room. What could I do at this time of night? I wanted to go along to Bénédicte's room,

but in the corridor I saw they weren't asleep yet, my mother and François. The strip of yellow light under the door. So, on tiptoe, I went back to the end of the corridor. They were in their room. I could hear their voices although I couldn't make out the words. I had a real urge to know what they were saying. It was too much for me. So I went into the bathroom, theirs, which led into the place where my mother keeps all her things—the dressing room it's called. I hid among the coats. From where I was I could hear snatches of what they were talking about.

"You're exaggerating," François was saying.

"Exaggerating? Why do you say I'm exaggerating?"

I stayed like that for a while. A spy in the closet. Basically. Then the voices stopped. The silence freaked me out. The flashbacks came back to haunt me. I was afraid of hearing suggestive noises. To calm myself down I thought: 'No, come off it, what are you dreaming up now? They're old, for Christ's sake. In their forties ... well, fifty in the handle's case. At that age you think about lots of things, but you don't think about that any more. You think about your work. You read the paper. You listen to classical music. But that, no'. I wanted to leave my hiding place and go back to my room, but suddenly the wardrobe door opened. I just had time to disappear into one of the furs that were hanging there. It was my mother. A few feet away from me. Stress. She was looking for something. She opened a few drawers. She looked livid. My heart was pounding. I was afraid she'd hear it. It was that loud, I'm telling you. If she found me here, you might say I was dead. Then François appeared behind her in the wardrobe doorway.

"Perhaps we should find a solution ... " he said.

"Oh yes? And which solution is that? Me, I've been looking for one for years, a solution."

"Why are you getting worked up?"

"Because I can't take it any longer. Do you understand?"

"See, you're at it again."

"I'm not at it again. I'm just telling you what I feel. Can't you see the atmosphere we're living in? I don't know, I've run out of patience."

"You only say that because you're afraid how he's going to react … "

"But I'm not asking his opinion on the matter. I'm not afraid of anything. It's my decision, isn't it? No, it's not that. The problem, I'm telling you, is that I've run out of patience."

My mother walked past him without looking round. François shut the door and followed her. I could still hear their voices. They were carrying on with the conversation in the next room. I was trembling. Without really knowing why. I got the feeling it was me they were talking about. She'd run out of patience? On account of me getting bad marks? Because I'd been caught smoking? Or was it that she'd noticed her photo was missing? Yeah, it had to be that. Shit. Suddenly I imagined the stupid bog not being able to completely swallow everything I put down it. Despite flushing it and everything. Maybe that was how she'd realised that I'd ripped up her photo? And why had I done it, anyway? I was torn: I was so freaked out about getting caught that I wanted to go back to my room, while at the same time my curiosity was getting the better of me.

So not to hide anything from you, I was in two minds whether to come out of my hiding place and tell them I knew all about it, the wedding business. Tell them they shouldn't worry about how I'd react, as Bénédicte had already spilt the beans. I was even on the point of telling them I thought it was a good idea, because I loved her. Yeah, I wanted to tell

her that, my mother. I'm telling you, I was as demented as that. But it must have been because of what I'd just heard. I was a child again, wanting to cry on her shoulder to be forgiven. Anyway. I went up to the door. She carried on: "I don't know what's happened. Before, he wasn't like this. He was more … I don't know. When I look at him, you know, I can't help thinking of his father. And the older he gets, the more like him he becomes. It's dreadful to say, but that's how it is. That same frightening face. For example, he's always telling lies. He never stops telling lies. And he steals money. Do you realise that? He steals in your house … "

"He's young," François tried to argue.

"It's got nothing to do with his age. There's more to it than it. I'm telling you, I've run out of patience. I can't stand it any more. He wears me out … because I know very well he does it to push me to the limit. Do you understand? Because he's got something against me. On account of his father and everything that happened back then. And after we're married it'll get worse and worse."

"That's why I'm saying that maybe we ought to find a solution … "

"What sort of solution?"

"Why not send him to his uncle's in Nice? Didn't he suggest it to you?"

"It's not possible. He's going to be travelling all year … Anyway, it's too complicated."

"There's always the possibility of that school we've talked about … "

"I know … "

I moved away from the door. I swallowed hard, it made my throat hurt. I went out of the dressing room via the bathroom. I didn't know what to do now. I stayed like that for a while, not moving. No idea. A bug. As if something

had just come apart inside me. It felt like someone had given me a great punch in the stomach. It had the same effect. I had trouble getting my breath back. Then I went back to my room. I locked the door. I sat on the bed. I breathed calmly, but I couldn't manage it. My hands were even shaking slightly. Not a lot, but slightly. I thought about what I'd just heard. I said to myself: What a bitch! She couldn't stand me any more. That's what she'd said. She thought I was getting more and more like my father, and she hated both of us. That was it: she hated us. Me, I hated her too. Everyone hated each other in this dump.

I'd never have believed she could talk about me like that. I knew she'd been through the mill because of me. I'd already heard her say on the phone that I was having a so-called difficult adolescence and that it was no picnic. But I never thought she'd say such lousy things about me. I swear to you. There must have been a mistake somewhere. I tried to work out what they meant. What was it, for example, this solution they had to find or something? The school … Suddenly I thought of Ben. A guy I often saw at my last school. Back then. Him too, he'd had problems with his parents because he didn't do any work in class and never stopped messing around. Well, his parents, they sent him off to a military boarding school mega-far away from Paris, in the Alps or something. A tough joint. Up at six and everything. With guys who were borderline illiterates. And monitor types who gave you a thrashing if you stepped out of line, and who apparently even slipped into your bed after dark. One day he came back to Paris during the holidays, Ben. We met up one afternoon and he told me about it. You'd have thought you were hearing things. According to him it was worse than hell. He looked really depressed. *Black Rocks*, it was called. A kind of prison. But not a prison

like the *Institute*. No. A real one. Without Madame Thomas.
Just for young people. Fuck. Maybe that was it, their idea.
To get rid of me. I knew my mother thought I created a
bad atmosphere at home. She'd criticized me about it tons
of times. If she sent me off to *Black Rocks* I'd be less of a
problem to her, that was for sure. At the time I panicked,
I can tell you. I had the feeling they were setting traps for
me, at night, the time when I was supposed to be asleep. I
felt betrayed. Still, I'd known for a long time I hadn't got
any well-wishers in this dump. You'd almost think they'd
have preferred to see me dead.

I stood up. Still shaking, I got undressed. I changed my
shirt, like. I still didn't know what I wanted to do, but it was
like a reflex: I had to escape. I got my black jacket from the
wardrobe. The one I love. I kept looking round in case I
forgot something important. I put a notebook and pencil in
my pocket. Then, on tiptoe, I went back to the bathroom.
Mine this time. I didn't want to turn the light on. Just in
case I was caught. I put on some deodorant. And a bit of
cologne. Some of the *Thé Vert* I'd asked for for Christmas. I
brushed my hair. It was strange to be doing these everyday
things when I was just beginning to understand what I was
about to do.

Then I went into the hall. Where the coats are kept.
I searched through most of the pockets. In François's
raincoat I found his wallet. All he'd done was just hang
up his things. I did a quick check. Fuck. No cash. So I
took his bank card. Too bad for him. It was perfect, the
card. I knew the PIN. I'd memorised it when he entered
it while I was next to him a few times. I was shaking. Yet I
wasn't afraid. It was just my hands, they were shaking by

themselves. Like mad. I wasn't in control. Again I thought about my mother who'd called me a thief, while I'd just found out she was going to marry this bloke for his money. It almost drove me nuts. Because telling a few porkies isn't necessarily any worse than saying to a guy "I love you" just for his money. It's always the guilty ones who point the finger at you. Anyway, who gives a shit! If they got married this money would come to my family. Bénédicte was going to be my stepsister? Well then, it was my step-money too. No reason to just have hassle. No reason to be shaking. After all, I was an adult now. I wouldn't let myself be sent to *Black Rocks* without doing something about it. I put the card in my inside jacket pocket. From that moment on I had no doubts. And, making as little noise as possible, I opened the door. Like a burglar, only in reverse. I went out. And just as carefully, on tiptoe, I shut the door behind me. My heart was pounding like someone trapped under the ice of a frozen lake. It went boom boom boom! Enough to wake the neighbourhood. Out on the landing, I wanted to use the lift for once. But I was afraid it would make too much of a row. So I went down the stairs. Flat out. To get outside as soon as possible. Into the mysterious night. Out of range. Out of reach.

PART TWO

DEPARTURE

1

I T WAS THE FIRST TIME I'd done that, leave in the middle of the night. For a second it fired me up, finding myself in that situation, but once I got down to the lobby of the building I had a moment of doubt. What was I going to do? It was true: I didn't even know where it was, Émilie Fermat's birthday party, except it was somewhere near the Champs-Elysées. Maybe I could call Marco? Or if the worst came to the worst, walk round aimlessly till dawn. But what would happen if I was caught? I'd be murdered in the morning. No doubt about it. And then they'd have every reason to send me off somewhere, like to *Black Rocks*. I had to face facts. If I left I couldn't come home again. It wasn't something to be taken lightly, some little escapade of running away. No. It was a whole lot more than that. I stayed in the lobby for a while, thinking. In fact, maybe it was better to go back to my room. Still, I'd got this far. The main door, that wasn't just nothing. I'd proved to myself that if I wanted to I could leave in the middle of the night. Okay. But now, maybe I shouldn't fool around too much. What's more I was beginning to feel tired … But I thought again about what I'd heard, everything my mother had said about me, that blow to the heart she'd given me, and it was enough to make me open the main door. What I felt wasn't just sadness, but a kind of mega-rage. I didn't have a choice. I had to leave, if possible for as long as possible. Not go for a walk round the neighbourhood, no. Leave.

The street was deserted. It must have been something like one o'clock in the morning. I wanted a smoke, just

to make me brave. But at the same time I was afraid of bumping into one of the neighbours. Fuck. The thought stressed me out again. Some character who'd recognize me and call the cops. My heart started drumming again. I had to calm down a bit or I'd drop dead from a heart attack tonight. The best thing was probably to clear off as soon as possible. I wouldn't run any risk on the Champs, for example, seeing my parents weren't the sort who knew the kind of people who go to the Champs in the middle of the night. The people my parents knew, most of the time, in the middle of the night they'd be asleep. Squares.

I headed for the métro, not quite running. There was no one in the street (except me). I was in a hurry to take off somewhere else. Without knowing why, it seemed the best idea. All the streets around the apartment building, they were still the same spider's web. My mother's. Especially if they'd maybe already realised I wasn't there, in my room … I imagined her doing a last walk round the apartment, like she often did before going to bed. Or getting up after hearing a suspicious noise in the hall when I closed the door behind me. It would have given her a shock to find my bed empty. She'd have understood the situation. But she'd have called the police immediately. That was just her style, my mother, to straightway pick the wrong solution. And so it goes without saying that it wouldn't take long to find me if I stayed in the neighbourhood. They'd bring me home by force. Or they'd take me down to the station to rot till dawn, which is what the law and fate have in store for a bad upbringing. Whatever the case, come Monday morning I'd be packed off to *Black Rocks*. To hell, you might say.

How could I avoid all that? Right at that moment I didn't really ask myself the question. I didn't have a plan. All I wanted was to escape. My idea was obviously to meet up

with Marco at Émilie Fermat's birthday party. It gave me an objective. Something concrete. And it gave me an excuse to not think too much about what I was letting myself in for. One thing at a time, I thought. First find them. Then we'll see. Suddenly I had an overwhelming sensation of freedom. I realised I could do anything I liked. Absolutely anything. I'd got money, thanks to the card. I was free. The idea of it made me feel happy, even if at heart I wasn't really happy, seeing I was sad. But still … For example, if I wanted to smoke I could draw out some money and buy cigarettes. Shedloads if that's what took my fancy. I imagined Marco's face when he saw me turn up at the party. It made me laugh already. He'd realise he'd made a slight mistake. It was a typical Marco-ism, that: you tell him that maybe you won't be coming to the party, and he straightway assumes your mother won't let you go out, as if you're still a baby. Marco, he always makes a point of treating other people like babies, just to make himself feel bigger. It's typical of him, that. But with the card, the flexible friend, I'd be able to turn up with a bottle, straight up. Real class. Champagne, if you like. Even a whole bottle, I didn't care: I wasn't going to let that stop me! I heard my laughter ring out along the avenue Mozart, which immediately scared the hell out of me because of all the echoes, and I speeded up again, turning right to the rue Fontaine.

The streets were barely recognizable compared with during the day. I looked round at all the sleeping buildings, home to hordes of people in slippers taking sleeping pills. A nasty neighbourhood, if you want my opinion. At this time of night there wasn't a light in any of the windows, and it gave me a strange feeling. As if they all lived in a gigantic dormitory. I imagined all these people lying side by side.

Waiting for the day they'd die. Most of them had no trouble getting to sleep. They weren't insomniacs or worriers. They didn't ask themselves too many questions. Just the ones that didn't upset them too much. Other questions, like why do we exist, they preferred not to ask themselves. For them and their sleep, a minute late was a minute too late. End of story. And anyway, they couldn't give a damn if life was a piece of crap and things were taking a turn for the worst. They'd rather go to bed to be on top form for the next day. So in contrast, that gave me even more the impression of being in the right place. Me, I didn't want to sleep.

Imagine a dog that you've tied to a post with a leash. Right. And one day, because of him pulling at it, imagine it breaks, the leash. Obviously the dog wouldn't want to sleep. Quite the opposite. He'd head off into the night like a lunatic.

I spotted the cash dispenser from a distance. It was shining. Like a lighthouse at night. So boats don't run aground on the rocks and get found with their hulls torn apart the next morning. Like hopes, a lot of the time. There was already a guy at the dispenser, putting in his code and virtually lying on top of the machine to stop prying eyes. A paranoid. I kept a few yards away from him. Just so as not to disturb him. Even so he still turned round, probably to see what I looked like. Thieves, you can tell them at a glance. Me, for example, at first glance you can see I'm no thief. But he still said "You got a problem?" "No" I replied straight off. And I looked away till he'd finished. The stress of my life. He shoved the money in his coat pocket. And he walked off, keeping close to the wall. A dodgy character, if you want my opinion.

I went and put in my card; well, François's card. I was

slightly wary. In case they had cameras and everything around cash dispensers. I put in the PIN as quick as possible. How much should I draw out? Maybe it was best not to get too much at once. It's not a good idea walking round at night with the entire contents of your bank account on you. Because holding up a guy is a breeze compared with holding up a bank. Okay. I selected forty euros, to start with. I looked to my right, to my left, to my right and again to the right, then to the left and finally to the right and left—just to see that no one was heading in my direction. Luckily the street was empty. I took back the card and the notes came out. There you go, Joe. I gulped, then shot off up the road, on the Périphérique side, because that's where the nearest métro station is; well, 'near' in a manner of speaking, because in this arrondissement everything is a long way from everything else. Nothing is nearby except the police station.

On the way I told myself that maybe it would be smarter to ring Marco right now rather than wait till I got there to find out where it was, Émilie Fermat's birthday party. But I didn't have a mobile or a phone card. So I carried on to the tabac and bistro on the corner of the rue La Fontaine, as I knew it was one of the last places in the world that still had payphones that took coins. My mobile, I'd lost it. It was my mother who first bought it for me, making out she was being kind, when I knew full well that to her mind it was actually so she could call me whenever she liked. With a mobile I was free on probation. But I did nothing but make calls, and every month, the bill, it went through the roof. It drove her crazy, my mother. In a sense I wasn't alone: all the guys my age did the same. But then I had it stolen. Or I lost it. Whatever, but it was two weeks now since I hadn't been able to make calls. It gave me the impression of being deaf-and-dumb.

As I walked I realised I'd never realised that the La Fontaine of the rue La Fontaine, was in fact the La Fontaine of the *Fables* by La Fontaine. Oh yeah … The one who wrote *The Cicada and the Crow*, for example. At night, some things leap out at you. Then I started dreaming: one day maybe there'd be a rue Julien-Parme. Or preferably an avenue. Because I like trees. People would stroll around there in melancholy mood. It's already a century since this author died and we still miss him just as much. Because I forgot to explain that I'm writing for posterity. Oh yeah. On François's building maybe there'd be a marble plaque and everything, with '*Julien Parme lived here*' written on it. A few young girls would be crying in front of it. The 'de', on the other hand, no one would talk about him. If you wanted to read a little plaque about him you'd have to go to the cemetery.

2

I WENT INTO THE BISTRO. It was virtually empty, obviously. Two guys were drinking at the bar. Most of the chairs had been upended on the tables. When it came to atmosphere it gave you a jolt. The barman glared at me. I asked him if he still sold cigarettes. He gestured at a packet of Lights. "That's all there is," he said. Marlboro Light, as a rule, I can't stand them. Because everyone smokes them. I swear to you. Okay, but I wasn't about to turn my nose up at them at one in the morning. So I got out a twenty euro note. Just like that. I even impressed myself. He gave me a dirty look, the barman. He mustn't have liked having to give change. So I added: "Could I have a beer as well?" Same thing, he didn't say a word. I went and sat at a table. After all, I'd got time. No need to change neighbourhood right away. Seeing I'd got the night ahead of me.

Suddenly I had this perfect idea. To write a novel called *The Night ahead of me*. The story of a guy who runs away. Hyper-original, that. Right. An Italian woman journalist knocks at the door of my office to ask me for a short interview. Usually I turn them down. But this journalist is a real beauty. I invite her in, glass of whisky in my hand. Very depressed. Very very. With dark rings under my eyes and everything. She follows me into my lair, rather overcome at the thought that it's here I produced my books. She sits in an armchair opposite me and immediately launches into the standard question: "Monsieur Parme, this amazing novel that's considered at an international level and

89

throughout the world as the greatest of the twenty-first century, I'm talking about *The Night ahead of me* of course, would it be right to say it's autobiographical?" I take a deep breath before replying. What's the point of all this palaver? Journalists' questions, in the end you know them off by heart. You know that the most important things lie elsewhere. Even if you have to play along with the media. "In the etymological sense, yes, you could say that. In the Greek sense, obviously … " After the interview I ask her what she's got planned. She replies, rather subtly: "Nothing. I've got the night ahead of me … " I give her a sad smile, and her too, she smiles, because she's realised that I'd like to find some consolation in her arms. To drive away, for a few hours, the desire to do myself in … Afterwards, she'd write her fucking article in the kitchen, naked. It would be on the front page of the paper in Italy, with my suicidal expression, my despairing look and my tobacco-stained fingers.

Just for that, I lit up. Dreamy and everything. I'd really like to be depressive … At that moment, as if they were reading my thoughts, the two guys sitting at the bar turned round, and then they laughed. What was wrong with me? It was probably my age. They must have been wondering what I was doing here, practically in the middle of the night. Then one of them whispered something in the barman's ear, who straightway turned and looked at me, as if to check, and then he laughed as well. They were up to something. Fuck. I began to freak out. Maybe they were saying I'd got money on me and everything. With three of them I didn't stand a chance. The barman finally brought me my beer. With the change. He still had a mocking expression, the great twat. What's more, you could bet your bottom dollar he'd never read a single one of La

Fontaine's fables and here he was coming the wise guy with me … To create a diversion I asked politely if there was a telephone. He nodded towards a door on the other side of the bar, near the bogs. Not much to say for himself, this bloke. Okay. I hadn't touched my beer, because I didn't much like the look of them, these characters. I got up to go and ring Marco. I put a euro in the slot and dialled. It gave me the feeling of being in an old film, a black and white one, because it was a phone that took coins.

I was afraid I'd get his voicemail, but luckily it rang. But it just kept on ringing. And in the end I got his voicemail. Shit. I hung up. He couldn't have heard his phone because of the music. I tried a second time. He still didn't answer. So I left a message: "Marco, yeah, it's Julien. What are you up to? I've been trying to get you for hours! Okay. Listen, I might come and join you … I wanted to know if it's any good, the party … Oh, and where it is … Because I forgot whereabouts … Émilie Fermat's address, like … So try and answer if you hear it ring. I'll call you back in half an hour. OK? The time it takes me to get to the Champs, alright. Bye then."

Next I called directory enquiries to get the Fermat's address, but the girl couldn't find anything under that name. Ex-directory, she told me. Ever since she'd been in that film, Émilie Fermat obviously thought she was Sharon Stone. She must have asked her parents to go ex-directory. Me, there's nothing that makes me more angry than that: if you've got a phone, it's so people can ring you, isn't it? Anyway, Émilie Fermat, she was the type who was really full of herself. The truth is that if she'd only been half as beautiful as she thought she was, she'd have had a lot of chances by now. Okay. But that's my opinion. And she liked to think she was mega-famous. Rubbish. If she'd

been famous, everyone would have known about it. If only by definition.

So then I went back into the main room, a bit worried and everything, and the guys at the bar started laughing again. Just to show them that their sarcasm didn't bother me, I finished my beer in one go. With the wine I'd drunk a bit earlier, my head was seriously beginning to spin. But not too much, though. Because I can hold my drink. As a writer, I mean. Then I had another idea. I should ring someone from my German class who might have the form list with them, and Mathilde's address as a result. Good plan. That's how I thought of Hervé Morvin.

Hervé Morvin, I'd better tell you right now, he was a real dipstick. I wouldn't have liked to be in his parents' shoes. Or his, either. What with his mug. And then he was always squealing on people, licking the teachers' boots and doing exercises that weren't asked for, or talking about books he'd supposedly read in the original German—basically, a total two-faced bastard. The proof was that instead of having a bag to put his school things in like everyone else, he carted a leather case around with him. The type bankers have. No, more like a minister actually. In it he had some sort of files. You got the impression he was running half of France, this bloke. He was so full of his own importance. Never would I have thought I'd be calling him at home. Which goes to show that life's full of surprises. I went back to the toilets. From directory enquiries I asked for Monsieur and Madame Morvin in Paris. They offered to put me through, and a second later it was ringing in my pal Hervé's apartment. I was mega-excited, convinced I'd had the idea of the century. It just shows I can't hold my drink as well as all that. Anyway.

A woman answered. In my best Jacques Chirac voice I asked if I'd got through to Madame Morvin.

"Who's speaking?"

"The President of the Republic," I nearly replied, doubled up with laughter. But suddenly, hearing her voice, I realised it was really late and that Morvin had probably been in his pit for years by now. I don't really know why, but I told myself I was going to get caught like a guy on the run, and anyway it was stressing me out and I hung up without answering. Then for a little while I stayed by the phone. I hesitated about whether to ring again. The excuse would have been to say we'd been cut off, bad connection and all that, and to get straight on to Morvin himself by insisting she had to wake him, something like: "It's a matter of life and death, madame ... " That made me laugh. Okay, but I wasn't too sure she'd got a sense of humour, Mother Morvin. So you could bet your bottom dollar I wouldn't get anywhere. In the end the idea of calling at this time, it wasn't a good one, not as an idea, but a bad one.

I went to check out the toilets. I quickly washed my face. There was a small mirror on the wall. That was when I realised. I still had the fucking lipstick on, which was trickling down my chin. It was probably why the two morons at the bar laughed when they saw me. I cleaned myself up with water from the tap. Lucky I'd seen it before meeting Mathilde Fermat. Because that, you might say it would have been the humiliation of my life. But was I even going to see her again? I hoped Marco would answer his fucking phone the next time I called.

I went back to the main room. The two guys stared at me. As I walked past them the little one with scruffy hair said, though I'm not sure I quite caught it: "You've cleaned yourself up then, sweetie." Very funny. No really,

very funny. I preferred not to reply. I don't take any notice of sarcasm. Like La Fontaine. Neither of us, we never talk to uneducated types. That's how it is. Question of principle, for a writer. "Yoo-hoo! I'm talking to you … " I pretended not to hear. I'm not joking. I sat down and lit another cigarette. Just to show them I didn't attach any more significance to them than the ant did to the fox in the fable (without wanting to show off my quotations too much).

Then I got up. "Oh! Leaving so soon … ?" It wasn't the moment to start getting involved in explanations that the lipstick, it was a misunderstanding. I thought it best to walk out of the bistro without batting an eyelid. A gentleman, even. I'm not the type to look for a fight, if you want to know. I'm anti-violence. Especially when it's just me against three blokes. I walked ten metres, and once I'd gone far enough I turned round and gave them the finger. Then I ran flat out without daring to look back. I stopped at the end of the street, completely out of breath. They'd had one too many, them. A couple of perverts, you could bet your bottom dollar. Okay. I went for a good ten minutes without seeing a single person. A desert. It was really strange to see the district so empty: it looked different at night. Then I got to the métro station. But it was closed. I remembered it didn't run all night. They had to get some sleep too, the drivers. So they'd be on form for the next strike. So there was only one other solution: take a taxi. As a rule I wasn't much used to taking them, taxis, but it was different now. I'd still got at least thirty euros on me. So I thought, fourteen-year-old guys, almost fifteen, with thirty euros in their pocket, there can't be a whole lot of them around at this time of night. Maybe I was the only one. That appealed to me, as an idea. Being the only one walking round in the open air

at night. Right. All the same I didn't want to be walking for hours. And I went and stood at a taxi rank, which was also deserted. No problem. I could wait. And I lit another cigarette, with a frown.

I waited, but there were no taxis in sight. If it went on like this I'd be going to Émilie Fermat's thirtieth birthday. I started getting impatient. So I decided to walk. After all, it wasn't that far, the Champs. I could cope with walking. And so that's how I set off for the Champs.

At one point, on a large avenue whose name I can't remember, I spotted a girl hanging around on the pavement. I straightway thought that maybe she was a professional, one from the back room if you see what I mean, and just at the thought of it I felt as if a fire had broken out in my guts. Huge flames were shooting right up my throat. It scared the hell out of me walking past her like that, so I wanted to cross the road, but that's when I saw there was another one just opposite. Fuck. I was surrounded. I tried to keep calm. But I couldn't, because now I'd got one to the right and one to the left, and my mind was full of all sorts of strange ideas. So I kept looking straight ahead, the unruffled sort of thing, all the while doing contortions with my eyes. A bit like a chameleon. So I could still eye them up. Because it rather fascinated me, all that sort of thing. Especially as I'd got some money on me for once.

It reminded me of the time, the year before, when I was walking around in Pigalle like a dog on heat. I was obsessed by what you could see there. I'd done it thousands of times: walk up the boulevard, then come back down, then go back up pretending I was in a real hurry and not even noticing that the street was swarming with peep shows. I was too shy to stop. I'd developed an ultra-specialized technique which let me letch in all directions while giving

the impression I was looking straight ahead. In fact it was the same technique I used in tests to copy my neighbour's answers. The chameleon technique.

As I passed the girl she didn't say anything at all. Straight up. It took my breath away. As if she'd asked me to make love with her. The stress of my life. So I speeded up the pace towards the Champs. (Marco, one time, he'd told me he'd tried it with a hooker. I swear to you. So not to take any risks, he used two condoms, one on top of the other. It had made me laugh, that little detail. One on top of the other. Because condoms, sometimes they burst without warning. Apparently. With that technique, Marco's, you were sure not to catch anything nasty. Cunning, eh? One on top of the other. Like wearing two pullovers on days when it's really freezing.) After about thirty metres or so I turned round. She was still waiting in the same place. And I said to myself that by paying a girl, maybe it was that too, that you paid, the thought that someone has waited for us in the cold, despite the darkness and the danger—the idea, even though it's an illusion, of someone waiting for you.

I walked for at least twenty minutes before catching sight of the Champs-Elysées. It was all lit up. You almost got the feeling it was early evening. Even the middle of the afternoon. The world back to front, like. I enjoyed seeing all that. I felt less alone. People were walking down the street. Some restaurants were still serving. The opposite of the Sixteenth, basically. I carried on until I got to the first pizzeria that was open. I told myself that a pizzeria probably has a payphone that takes coins. No doubt you're wondering why. The answer's simple: pizza, it's mostly for poor people. So are payphones that take coins. Elementary

... Anyway. That's what I thought in the midst of the insomniac waves of people who weren't asleep yet, despite the time, although I imagine it wouldn't be long before they were, seeing it was already mega-late—and I take the opportunity to dedicate these words to the Académie Française.

Here I am.

The Champs, it's not at all what you think. I wouldn't want to flaunt my learning by quoting too much, but someone, a Polish writer from the last century, said it was the most beautiful avenue in the world. I don't agree with him at all. But to my mind, the man who said that, the Pole, he thought the same as me, even if he wrote the opposite. Only he told himself that if everyone repeats it, we'd be rid of the Japanese and the grockles. Because obviously, the Japanese and the grockles, you tell them it's the most beautiful avenue in the world and immediately they show up there. It's like a reflex. And so you can stroll around the nicer parts of Paris without having them disturb you. Saint-Sulpice for instance. That's what I think anyway.

And Mathilde, was she really going out with that bastard Marco?

In the pizzeria I straightway asked one of the waiters if there was a payphone that took coins, but the guy walked right past me without replying. Typical Italian behaviour. All the same, and I'd rather say this straight out, even if it's got nothing to do with anything, I love pizza. Anyway. I stood waiting in the middle of the restaurant like a twat for a few minutes, thinking he'd be back to give me an answer once he'd put down his plates and everything. Then I got sick of waiting. So I went for a look round the bogs. It was sort of my speciality tonight, bogs. I searched everywhere, but no phone. Shit. On the other hand, and this made

97

me laugh, there was a condom machine and a guy whose coins had apparently been swallowed by it. Furious and everything, he was thumping away at this machine which had him by the dick. Maybe he hadn't got any more coins, I thought, and his girlfriend was waiting for him at the table over there, not knowing what he was plotting. Me, if I was meeting a girl for dinner, I'd never take her to a crap restaurant like this. I was in two minds whether to offer him a euro in exchange for making a call on his mobile. These days everyone's got a mobile, except me, who's had it stolen. But in the end I didn't say anything, out of shyness. And I went back to the main restaurant.

I didn't quite know what to do now. And that's when the first unlikely thing of the evening happened: at a table at the far end I spotted Madame Thomas, my French teacher. I swear, I'm not making it up. Madame Thomas, in person. I hesitated for a second. Perhaps I'd do well to hide, seeing after all I was a runaway. But I stayed there, looking at her. Like in front of a landscape.

She was on her own. Oh my God, I thought. In fact it had never really registered with me that she also had a life outside school. In hindsight, I think that by standing without moving like that, I was waiting for her to turn round and see me first. In any case, I didn't know what else to do. I had nowhere to go. Then I remembered the first time I'd seen her, Madame Thomas. It was three weeks after the *rentrée*. Originally, as I've already told you, it was Monsieur Vigouse who was supposed to be teaching us. But he'd had an accident. We never found out what kind. We were all jumping for joy, when he might have been run over by a métro train. (Teachers, anyway, the only time they make people happy is when they're ill. Lessons get cancelled.) There was a rumour that he'd been mown

down by a car while walking along the street minding his own business. Death, it could come at any moment. We shouldn't ever forget that. But too often we behave as if we've got plenty of time ahead of us. We stroll down the street, whistling.

Anyway. For a week after Monsieur Vigouse went we didn't have French lessons. And then it was on that Monday that she appeared, Madame Thomas. She straightway fascinated me. She walked up onto the platform, mega-calm and everything, in a skirt and her see-through blouse, she put down her things and announced: "Right. As from today it's me who'll be looking after you." That staggered me, as an approach.

After a while standing still in the middle of the Italian restaurant, she turned round and our eyes finally met. She gave me a big smile, a really friendly smile, but at the same time I sensed she was embarrassed and that she was wondering what the hell I was doing there. It's true it was an unlikely situation. I walked over to her, in a shy sort of way.

"Hello, Julien," she said. "What are you doing here?"

Madame Thomas, she was the only one who called you '*vous*'. The other teachers called you '*tu*' all the time just to appear pally, when the truth was they swore about you.

"I'm going to a party," I replied, proudly.

I was in luck: for once I was going to a party and she was there to take note of it. I added, just to impress her a bit more: "On the Champs … " But then I suddenly realised that perhaps I ought to have lied. On account of having run away.

"But haven't you got school tomorrow?"

As she said it she looked at her watch. She must have forgotten it was a staff training day. That's what I told her. Then I immediately added, so as not to talk too much about school any more.

"And you, you had dinner here?"

She gave a funny little smile.

"Yes."

"Ah? You like pizza?"

"No, not really."

What else could I say? I tried to think of a topic of conversation? A literary subject. Or the title of a novel. Something to create a good impression. And a diversion. But I couldn't think of anything. In the meantime I said: "Me neither, pizza, it doesn't really appeal … " Then I lit a cigarette. I offered her one. She seemed to hesitate. In my opinion she felt awkward taking one from one of her pupils. I nearly told her I was giving up my studies. To put her at ease, over the cigarette. But I didn't need to: in the end she took it. That threw me, to be honest. Straightway I lit it, her cigarette.

"And you, you had dinner here too?"

I imagined myself telling her that actually I'd only come in to find a payphone, just to make a call (logical), because I'd had my mobile pinched in a pretty nasty fight that I'd come out of quite well, given the number of guys who'd jumped me, even if I hadn't managed to not lose my mobile, as well as a bit of blood on the bridge of my nose (nothing serious luckily), but that in fact I hadn't been able to find a phone in this restaurant, but that, in spite of everything, if she wanted she could come with me to this girl Émilie Fermat's birthday party. Oh my God! Marco's face! I'd have really liked to see it. But in the end I opted for a less original answer:

"Er, no, I was looking for a phone actually … I've absolutely got to call some friends. And I was hoping there'd be one in this restaurant."

She offered to let me use her mobile. Straight up. Which proves how decent a teacher she really was. Always thinking of how to help her pupils whenever she could. I accepted, a bit overcome. But at the same time I didn't want to go at all. I'd have liked to stay like that for hours, opposite her, looking at her. Discussing literature. Or crying on her shoulder, telling her about everything that had just happened to me. I dialled Marco's number. Suddenly I heard his voice. Alleluia. But my heart wasn't in it any longer.

"Hello?"

" … "

"Hello?"

" … "

He couldn't hear anything because of the music.

"Can you hear me?"

"Yeah, yeah, that's it … Who's that?"

"It's me."

"Who's that?"

"It's Julien!"

I felt awkward. I didn't really want Madame Thomas to hear. But at the same time I had to yell because of the music. What's more, the whole restaurant could hear what I was saying, I was yelling so loudly.

"Listen, I've got to go to another party now, with some famous friends, but I'd still like to drop in and say hi before heading off elsewhere … "

"But you're where, now?" Marco shouted.

"Eh? On the Champs … "

"Oh? And you're going to come?"

"Yeah … Just to say hi. Because then I've got this other

thing. A party with some writer friends."

A glance at Madame Thomas to savour the effect.

"What? Okay. So you're coming! Are you on your own or with Charlotte?"

"A sort of symposium about Kafkaf."

Another discreet glance.

"Sorry?"

"Exactly. For the review I write for regularly."

"What are you talking about?"

"No, no, under a pseudonym."

"I can't understand a thing you're on about, Jules."

"Uh-huh."

"Right. Listen then, it's rue Pierre-Charron. You know it?"

"Uh-huh."

"You hear me? Number thirteen. No need for a code. Just press the buzzer marked Fermat. How's it going?"

"Uh-huh ... very interesting."

"OK? Right. It's cool you can come! We'll have a great laugh! You'll see! There are some bombs here! Yee-ha!"

"I understand. I'll talk to my publisher about it."

"What?"

"Not at all. See you later."

I hung up, pleased with my masterstroke. She was looking at me in an odd way now. I thanked her for the phone. It was really kind of her. I wanted to listen to my voicemail as well, but then I'd have felt I was taking advantage. Besides, I wasn't quite myself any more. My heart was pounding. Even so, I was with Madame Thomas in a restaurant on the Champs at one in the morning—although without any ulterior motives. I couldn't get over it. In a little while, perhaps we'd be out in the street. Everything would seem beautiful to me, even the bare trees sticking up miserably from the concrete.

I'd offer to take her home in a taxi, to drop her off at her place, even to let her get close to me when it came to saying goodnight, to get closer, closer, as if to kiss each other, but so that our lips brushed, so that we kissed with our tongues and everything, and then she'd suggest I came up, to her apartment—needless to say to her bedroom—and we'd find ourselves in a lift that was too small for my love, and we'd kiss again, again, right up to the moment we slipped into her bed where I'd recite some poetry, but not only that.

What does a woman of her age think about? I mean, a woman of at least thirty. Some nights does she dream about sleeping with a guy of fourteen, soon to be fifteen? Because me, you might say I've spent thousands of hours in the imaginary arms of women that age. I know it happens sometimes. In my opinion female paedophilia should be encouraged. Especially as Madame Thomas had fantastic eyes. I told myself I ought to try something. In my dreams. I could suggest we go for a drink somewhere. At her place, for example. If she wasn't sure, I could tell her the truth: it was maybe the last time we'd see each other, seeing I wasn't planning on coming back to the *Institute* and that I'd run away. But I was too strung out for that, obviously. In Pigalle I daren't even stop at a peep show … So to suggest something like that to a real woman, I didn't even think about it. Well yes, actually, I did think about it, but knowing I'd never be brave enough to do it.

To get the conversation going again, as well as to justify standing in front of her doing nothing, I asked if she enjoyed it at the *Institute*. It was either that or the weather, and me, I don't know a thing when it comes to the weather.

"Quite. And you?"

"Me?"

"Yes. Do you enjoy it there?"

I was afraid of putting my foot in it. I remained cagey.

"Not really. Most of the lessons, I find them boring. Except French, that's my favourite subject."

She smiled. I got the feeling she was making fun of me slightly, as if I was saying that to suck up to her. Still, she only had to check my report: apart from in French I did zilch. So I tried to be more specific:

"It's the only subject that has anything to do with everyday life. I find. That's what I like about literature."

"You read?"

"I never stop," I replied, puffing as if it wore me out physically.

"Oh? What sort of books?"

"It's books about despair that I find most moving actually."

"Books about despair ... Why?"

Another amused little smile. I straightway regretted having said it.

"Me, I'm more of an optimist and all that, but when you read a book about happiness, with a false ending where everything ends well, you get the feeling of being excluded from it, from the happiness. While it's the opposite with a book that's really despairing, I don't know, you find someone who suffers like you do, who has the same sorrows, a sort of brother like, and that makes things a bit less bad."

I'd spouted all that out without thinking, and I was scared stiff of her reaction. She looked at me strangely, on account of the spiel I'd just given her, so I added: "But I like books with happy endings too." And as I had the feeling I was looking like a prat, I ended by saying: "Okay, but it depends." Before qualifying it one last time by adding the classic: "Actually, I don't know ... "

At that moment the guy from the toilets came up to our

table. The one from the condom machine. I wondered
what he wanted. Madame Thomas introduced us. It
was her bloke. I swear to you. I was mega-embarrassed.
Especially as he was at least forty. Maybe even older.
Suddenly I felt worthless. He looked at me as if I was a
turd on the pavement. I nearly offered to lend him a coin,
for the machine, while asking if it didn't make him feel
uncomfortable to be quietly planning to screw the woman
in my life. But I realised I had to leave them. Him too, he
looked surprised to see me still up at this time of night. As
if I was twelve. That really annoyed me. Adults, most of
the time they don't have a clue about anything. In any case,
him, he didn't imagine for a minute that I could be a rival,
that I was a man too, and that frankly it was depressing to
look at me as if I was a child who should have really been
in his pyjamas, seeing what time it was.

So, a bit melancholy and everything, I said goodbye to
her, to Madame Thomas, as solemnly as possible. I wanted
her to understand it was a last goodbye, an adieu. Because
obviously I wouldn't be able to come back to the *Institute*.
Given the situation. But that, she couldn't know that yet.
She'd miss me. She seemed troubled. As if she'd realised
it could have worked out between us. Then I thanked
her for lending me her phone. I left the restaurant full of
conflicting emotions. It was strange. I didn't know what to
think any more. In the street I closed my eyes to make sure
I fixed the last image I'd have of her in my mind. After all,
she'd taught me a lot. Everything I'd written, for example,
it was to please her that I'd made so much effort to do it.
But I had to face facts: I was fourteen, going on fifteen.
I didn't measure up. Not yet. Then I said to myself: "It's
crazy all the same, running into her like that in the middle
of the night. Right in the middle of Paris. It's really an

amazing coincidence … " It's true when you think about it: it was crazy. But coincidence, me, I don't believe in it. And La Fontaine, did he believe in it, coincidence, I wondered as I set off again? Probably not. As a writer, I mean. He must have believed in destiny more than anything, I think. Like me. Anyway, most of the time it's simple: La Fontaine and me, we agree about everything. Especially him.

3

AﬆFTER THAT I WALKED to the rue Pierre-Charron. I was
still fairly excited from meeting Madame Thomas. But
also because it was quite new for me to be trailing round like
this in the middle of the night. I got the impression everyone was looking at me and thinking: 'Him, he's still up at
this time of night?' But I knew that no one actually noticed
me. I tried not to think too much about what I was doing.
Because deep down I was aware I was fooling around at the
very limit of how far you can fool around. What was going
to happen in the morning? I thought that maybe François
would cancel his bank card when he realised I'd nicked it.
The solution, which I hadn't thought of till just now, was
to draw out some reserves tonight. A gold mine all at once.
If not, I'd pretty soon find myself with nothing. And then
I'd have to go home. Or find a job so I could live and, since
I haven't got a driving licence yet, I'd end up working at a
supermarket checkout. Right then: next cash machine, that
was for me.

I stopped outside number thirteen. The main door was
open. Inside there was a sort of courtyard. The inner
courtyard, I suppose. Okay. I went across it. I straightway
spotted where the party was. Music was spilling out of the
windows on the sixth floor. It was so loud it made your ears
hurt. It made you want to suggest having a minute's silence,
if only for the neighbours' sake. But maybe she'd invited
them, the neighbours, Émilie Fermat, to get them on her
side. Or they daren't say anything just because she'd already

been in a film and was quite well known. People are stupid enough for that. Especially if they're your neighbours. Anyway. I looked for the name 'Fermat' on the entryphone. Then I buzzed. While I waited for a reply, it crackled. To tell the truth I was a bit stressed, because I knew virtually no one at this party, me. There'd just be final years and film actors. In a way I didn't give a toss, seeing that me, if I was coming, it wasn't for them but for Mathilde. Okay. But all the same ... Besides, Marco would be there. I wouldn't be on my own. So no problem. I buzzed again.

"Yeah? Hello? Who is it?"

A woman's voice. It must have been Émilie. Shit. I'd have rather got someone else. Because Émilie, I didn't much like her. I swallowed before giving my name.

"It's Julien."

" ... "

"Julien Parme."

"Who?"

"Julien Parme."

"It's who? Julien Barme?"

"Parme. I'm a friend of Marco's."

"Eh?"

"A friend of Marco's. And Mathilde's."

"Oh yeah ... it's on the sixth."

"On the sixth floor?" I asked, to lighten the atmosphere.

"What?"

"On the sixth what? The sixth floor?"

She didn't see the funny side of it.

"Are you stupid or what? Not the sixth floor of the basement," she replied really abruptly and then pressed the button.

I'd rather botched the introductions. But the main thing was she'd let me in. Okay. I took a deep breath before

opening the door. Now it was just a matter of climbing the stairs. Suddenly I remembered I hadn't brought a present. Fuck. I hadn't even given it a thought, me, that it was a birthday party. I hadn't really been expecting to come. That's just how it had turned out. I started having qualms. She'd think I was taking advantage. And then she'd tell Mathilde. Shit. I had to find something ... I looked round. Between the dustbins and the staircase there was a door, probably leading down to the cellar. I thought of taking a quick look down there and maybe pinching something. It was a good idea. Sometimes you find some fantastic things in cellars. As long as I didn't go thieving in the Fermat's cellar. Because if I gave them something that already belonged to them, on top of the joke that fell flat it could cause a bit of a frost. I tried the door but it was locked. Damn. I was going to force it open but it was the type where you couldn't do that. I'd have to find something else.

That's when I had an idea. I went back the way I came, wedging the door open with the mat so I could get back in. I didn't want to end up outside again. The doormat was perfect. It was really stiff and everything. No problem. In the inner courtyard I went over to one of the windows on the ground floor. My heart started pounding flat out. There was a pot of geraniums on the ledge. Well okay, it's not the best present in the world. But it's still a present. Besides, girls, they like that, flowers. Roses, tulips, geraniums, it's the same thing. Or almost. You water them and then they wilt. Okay. That way she could put them on her windowsill. She'd understand that this present, you had to take it slightly tongue-in-cheek. I looked round ... I went up to the flower pot ... When suddenly I heard a noise behind me which made me jump more than ever! I came close to having a

heart attack. Serious. I headed back to the entrance hall. Fuck. The door had shut by itself. The mat hadn't held. Shit. Okay. I went over to the ground floor window again. In a flash I pinched the pot of flowers. Then I went back to the entryphone. I buzzed again, making sure there was no one behind me. I hoped I'd get someone else this time. But no, it was still Émilie who answered. Fuck, it was her birthday and she had nothing better to do except pick up the entryphone …

"Yeah?"

I cleared my throat slightly and scratched my nose.

"Er … It's Julien again."

"What?"

It's true you couldn't hear a thing over the music.

"It's Julien again."

"Julien who?"

"Julien Parme. Marco's friend."

"Ouf, I've just let you in … Didn't it work?"

I thought it was a chance to make up for my crap joke from just now.

"Yes, yes … But I went down to the sixth floor of the basement and there was no one there."

" … "

"Hello?"

" … "

"Hello?"

" … "

I heard a voice in the distance: "Here, you take it, it's your mate, you sort it out with him, we're not really getting through to each other the pair of us … "

"Hello? So what the hell are you up to?"

"Nothing. I'm downstairs. Can you let me in then?"

"Yeah. Just a sec … Is that okay?"

The metallic buzzing sound rang out.

"Fine. I'm on my way up."

All the same I was relieved it was him I'd see first when I got to the apartment. It would be easier. Because at that moment, you could say I had the feeling that I hadn't got a clue what I was doing. As a rule I don't give a toss, me, about Émilie Fermat. But it would still have annoyed me if she told her sister I was an idiot and everything. At the same time it's not my fault if she hasn't got a sense of humour or anything. Émilie, she took herself too seriously in my view. If you take yourself seriously, it's got to be because you overestimate how much longer we've got to live. I know that because I read it somewhere.

As I went up the stairs I met two policemen. I swear to you. They were coming down quite calmly. I nearly turned and legged it that instant. Like a reflex. Even if I knew they weren't there because of me. But when you do something stupid like run away from home, you're bound to get the impression that people are lying in wait for you on every street corner. One of the policemen said good evening as he looked me up and down. I replied in my out-of-control voice, hiding the flowerpot behind my back. I didn't look too clever, I can tell you. And straightway I thought, if my mother finds out I'm not there, if she wakes up or something, the first thing she'll do is ring Émilie Fermat's place. Seeing she knew I'd originally been planning on going to her birthday. I imagined the cops turning up in the middle of the party and asking if there was a Julien Parme among the young people. It scared the hell out of me, thinking that, and I almost told myself it wasn't really a good idea to go to this party. But the truth is, it was more than anything because I was stressed. Over Mathilde and everything. On the sixth floor I had one last hesitation

111

about the pot of flowers. In the end, Émilie, she wasn't the type to like flowers. She was more the type to take the piss out of me. I didn't want people saying afterwards that I'm romantic and everything. So I thought it best to put the pot down. Outside the neighbour's front door. I rang the bell. The door opened straight away.

"How's it going?"

It was Marco.

"And you?"

"It's cool. Come on in. So you could finally make it?"

I was still really pleased to show him it was a yeah. The proof:

"Yeah."

That shut him up a bit.

"So you dumped that girl in the end?"

"Which girl?"

"The girl you had a date with."

"Which one?"

"The one you had a so-called date with … "

I didn't know if he believed my story about Charlotte. Because he had a glint in his eye whenever he mentioned it. Still, that was too bad: I was here and he couldn't say anything.

"I didn't dump her," I replied. "It's just that I wanted to spend a bit … And Mathilde?"

"What?"

"She's here?"

"Yeah. Why?"

I straightway told him I wanted to talk to him about something, just him. Something mega-important. Private, like. Without really believing me he said to follow him. We walked down a long corridor. Everyone in the living room. And the room next to it. As we went past

the doorway I saw that not many people were dancing. Most of them were sitting talking, taking it easy Miami-style. Funny sort of atmosphere, I commented. Some of the guys were maybe about twenty. Even older. So Marco told me the police had suddenly arrived just before I did. Apparently because it was late and you weren't allowed to make so much noise after a certain time. Disturbing the peace, he explained, with the grin of a specialist in such things. And at night too. The neighbours had been complaining. And so they'd had to turn the volume right down. It had killed the atmosphere stone dead. Which was really rather a shame. Especially for a birthday party. "It's stupid," I said, to make him think I felt concerned, but the truth was I was looking round everywhere to see where Mathilde was. The idea, so things didn't go flat, was to move on to a nightclub.

"Oh, really?"

Me, nightclubs weren't quite my thing. Especially as I wasn't sure I'd be able to get in. Given my age. And it would have really done my head in if a bouncer had said "no, not you" in front of the others. Plus embarrassment into the bargain.

"Yeah. Émilie knows a really good place, from what she says. We're going to make a move any minute."

At the end of the corridor we went into a bedroom. The spare room, I imagine. It was where you left your coat and stuff, but me, my black jacket, the one I love, I preferred to keep it on. Suddenly Marco remembered I'd got something important to tell him.

"So? What is it?"

Deep down I didn't really know what I wanted to ask him. If I told him straight out that my mother wanted to marry François, he wouldn't have understood where I was coming

from. That wasn't the best approach to take. Besides, as for the business with Mathilde, I wasn't sure how to raise the subject again. I wasn't about to suddenly tell him I was crazy about the girl … he'd have taken the piss out of me. And then what else? The fact that I'd just run into Madame Thomas, that was something I'd also have liked to tell him, even if he'd never have believed me. Not forgetting the fact that I'd cleared off from home. In short, I'd got thousands of things to tell him. But I wasn't sure where to start. Just at that moment, that's to say just as I was about to spill it all to him, Émilie Fermat came in. Marco introduced us. Hi, hi. She gave me a kiss without really looking at me. I forgot to wish her happy birthday. Then she told Marco there was something she absolutely had to show him. He said okay, the bastard, and the pair of them walked out. Without me. "I'll be back in a sec … " As she went out she switched off the light, as if she'd forgotten I was there, I swear to you, and I found myself in darkness. Right, okay, nice.

While I waited for him to come back, I went to the living room to give it a scan. But from a distance. I felt rather self-conscious, although not so much now. There were loads of people, all older, but to hell with them. I headed straight for the table where there were bottles of champagne. Just champagne. But they were all empty. One thing was for sure, they hadn't waited for me before they started drinking. Some guy said they'd gone to get some more from the kitchen. Cool. While I waited I sat down. Okay. Now I could do that trick of the guy who launches into an enormous great description of the party. But I'd already read Balzac, the bloke who wrote *L'Assommoir*, and I'm not that much of a sadist to force reams of detail down your throat. I'm

well aware that this party, you obviously don't want to know everything about it: like how many ashtrays there were on the little table to the right of my chair—that sort of thing. Because in the end, this party, you don't give a damn about it. Besides, you weren't invited. It's me who dragged you along. I assume. So I'll keep it brief. The only thing worth knowing is that I was wondering more and more what I was doing here. I was out of place and I felt minute. Transparent. And superfluous. Like a nit on a bald head.

Sitting next to me was a blonde girl. Mega-tall, actually. But that's alright, she was sitting down. Okay. Maybe it was stupid, but I couldn't resist, I asked what her name was.

"Marion," she replied, and then turned away.

But I kept up the attack. I asked if I could just have a sip from her glass. Because I was dying of thirst. I swear to you. And all the bottles were empty. I know it's not the sort of thing you say, but her drink, I got the impression she hadn't touched it for hours, and that she wouldn't ever finish it anyway. Otherwise I wouldn't have dared. She gave me a funny look before replying, quite subtly: "That bothers me, because then you'll be able to read my thoughts … " On account of the saying. I thought that was pretty classy. So I waited for the bottles to arrive from the kitchen.

After ten minutes I was still in the same place and I still hadn't said a word to anyone. Even so I had a big smile on my face, the laid-back sort, although slightly forced so it wasn't too obvious that I was feeling ill at ease. In any case, no one seemed to have noticed me. I wondered where Marco was. As I lit a fag, I said to myself that in fact I did want to confide in him. At the same time I couldn't quite see me telling him everything regarding my running away. I preferred it if he thought he'd been mistaken about me, and that I wasn't the type to get punished by my mother,

etc. But as I was thinking that, I was also thinking the opposite. Maybe he could give me some advice about what I should do now. For example: where was I going to sleep tonight? My first thought was obviously to go to his place. It was odd in a way, since I'd been hating him all evening because of the trick he'd played on me over Mathilde. But I'd almost forgotten that now. Because all that mattered to me at that moment was telling him how I'd done a bunk. I needed to do it. In fact, I think I was feeling a bit lost. In one way I was glad to be here. But in another I had the feeling that I was going to regret it.

From what I could work out, my mother had asked my uncle if I could go and live with him in Nice. He had said no. I understand. The problem is that he was my only family. My mother, she didn't have a brother or any relatives. As far as I knew she had had one once, but he'd died when they were small. In an accident. She never talked about it. And then I'd lost both my grandmothers. It was really bad luck. On my father's side there was my uncle. But he didn't have children. In short, if I left my mother I'd end up without a family. Basically. That was what it was, the solitude I was feeling. It gave me stomach ache, as if I'd swallowed a nail. Marco, even though he wasn't one of my family, I was happy being with him. In a way he reassured me. Because he was far from stupid, Marco. Even if he sometimes got close to it.

But he didn't come back. And Mathilde was still nowhere to be seen. More and more I was wondering if I'd done the stupidest thing in my life by coming here. I looked round: frankly there was nothing of great interest. It wasn't exactly the high life, this party of theirs. Okay, there was

champagne and everything. But I don't know: the people all looked so stupid. And happy to be. Besides, I was dreading the cops would suddenly turn up. I swear to you. I couldn't get the idea out of my mind. They'd put the cuffs on me and all that. I hoped at least that Mathilde would see it all. Maybe the best thing was to leave right away. It's true, with the money from François's card I'd be able to do what I wanted. So why stay at this party? I was sure there were plenty of fascinating things that happened in Paris at night. You just had to walk round and run into some good people. Me, what I'd have loved is to have incredible adventures. I hadn't given it enough thought, but if needs be, with money, I could even get a train ticket and split, go really far away. To Italy for example. With Marco. We'd leave tomorrow, after going to the bank to draw out a stash. We'd treat ourselves to a month of peace, quiet and happiness. Instead of going to stupid parties. With people who are happy to be the same. Thinking about it did me good. It wasn't just the night I had ahead of me but my whole life. To celebrate I wanted a drink. Okay. But since we were still waiting for them, the famous bottles from the kitchen, but also to fool around, I turned to my blonde neighbour.

"What are you thinking about?" I said.

She had been looking vacant for some time now, Marion. "What?"

"What are you thinking about?"

"Nothing," she replied, a bit surprised by the question.

"So I can have some of your drink then … "

She looked at me as if I was from another planet. Then she laughed. What's more, I'd said it seriously. But she thought I had a quick sense of humour. Compared with the way she replied the first time.

"What's your name?"

"Julien."

"Are you a friend of Émilie's?"

"Vaguely … "

"But how old are you?"

At the time it annoyed me, as a question.

"Sixteen. Why?"

"No reason."

She stood up. It was like Everest. Then she handed me her glass: "Here, go on, I've finished, me." She went out and headed for the bedrooms. And I finished it off in one go, the glass.

As I drank I gave more thought to the idea of asking Marco if I could crash at his place for the night. There was room for two in his bedroom. But at the same time it was dicey. My mother, it would be the first place she'd come looking for me in the morning. When she got up and saw I hadn't slept at home, she'd charge straight round to Marco's. To find out where I was hiding. No doubt about it. So it wasn't possible. What would have been good, I thought as I emptied my glass, was if my father had still been alive. I'd have gone to his place and explained that I'd had an argument with my mother. He'd have understood, him, seeing that at the time he did nothing but argue with her. He'd have approved. And I'd have been able to sleep at his place. Okay, he'd have bollocked me a bit for running off in the middle of the night, but gently. Just a bit, so I didn't do it again. If needs be I'd have moved in with him for good. In his apartment. That's where I'd have written my novel. Literature, he knew all about it, he did, seeing he used to be a journalist. A journalist and a writer, that's almost the same profession. Not really the same, since it's

exactly the opposite. But almost. Anyway, if he'd still been alive he'd have been pleased, my father, to know I wrote books.

Marco finally came back into the living room. I straightway went up to him.

"What the hell have you been doing?"

"I'll tell you," he replied with an air of mystery.

"Go on, tell me … "

"I'm on to something."

"A girl?"

"Yeah. And a real bomb."

Obviously I was intrigued. "Come on, I'll show you." He took me by the arm and led me towards the kitchen. He looked really excited. Was he talking about Mathilde? On the way he shook hands with three guys who behaved as if I wasn't there.

"Do you know who that was?" he asked me after he'd exchanged a couple of words with a bloke.

"Who?"

"Ouf, the bloke I was just talking to … "

"No. Who was it?"

He came out with a name I hadn't heard of and which I've since forgotten. I think it was an actor who'd been in Émilie Fermat's film. Someone else who thought he was famous. Rubbish. When a guy's famous but no one knows, it's simply because he isn't famous. Logic. I raised my eyebrows insincerely to show that it impressed me. He was pleased with himself, Marco, for having spoken to this guy I pretended to recognize in front of me. It delighted him.

"Come on, it's this way … "

He was guiding me as if he was at home.

"It's huge, their apartment … "

"You don't say. It's their father's."

"Their parents are divorced?"

"Ouf, yeah. Like everyone's … "

He could talk, he could. Not only were his parents still together, but on top of that they lived in Morocco. Supposedly.

"Where are we going then?"

"You'll see."

We stopped at the end of the corridor. He knocked on a door. We went into the bathroom. A guy and two girls had shut themselves in to get some peace and quiet. The bath was full of ice to keep the bottles cool. It was the bottle stash, like.

"What do you want?" the bloke asked.

One of the girls, the dark-haired one, you could see her nipples through her top. You could bet your bottom dollar that that was Marco's plan.

"Go on, crack open the champagne."

He popped a cork.

"In the living room," I said, "they're all waiting for more bottles."

That made everybody laugh, although there was nothing funny about it. I was informing them, that's all. But them, information, it made them laugh. Don't ask me why. Okay. And that's when I got a shock. The bloke in front of me, he was the spitting image of Yann Chevillard. But I couldn't work out if it was actually him or not. Yann Chevillard, he was the guy I'd been planning to see again for years so I could smash his face in. After all the lousy tricks he'd played on me, I'll tell you. Meanwhile we were short of a glass. I said I'd go and get one, and I went out of the bathroom, still with the nasty feeling that maybe I'd met up with that turd Chevillard again. I went back down the

120

long corridor to the living room. And there, getting herself a drink, not in the living room but in the next-door room, I at last saw Mathilde. It stressed me out. Like having a vision. I wanted to backtrack. Or hide. But at the same time, that was what I was here for. To see her. It wasn't the moment to chicken out. Quite the opposite. Especially as it was maybe the last time I'd see her. Given my situation. I went and stood next to her. Okay. It was at least a minute before she noticed I was there.

"Oh, hi," she said.

"Hi."

I'd replied really coolly, but without meaning to.

"They're empty," I added, pointing to the bottles, just to break the ice.

She smiled, and then moved away. Shit. I took a sip from my empty glass, to give myself time to think of another idea. With all the alcohol I'd drunk, I was getting slightly out of my box. She sat on her own near the window. At any rate, she didn't know anyone either, I thought. It was just her sister's birthday, not hers. She seemed as bored as I was. Looking at her like that, by the window, it occurred to me that she was the opposite of her sister. They were nothing like each other, the two of them. You wouldn't have thought they had the same mother. If you want my opinion, for two sisters it was strange how they didn't look anything like each other. Especially Mathilde.

I headed back to the bathroom with my glass. Once I got there, Marco filled it to the top. We drank a toast. The dark-haired girl's nipples were still sticking out. You'd have thought she was doing it deliberately, just to turn you on. A tease, like. I sounded out the guy who I'd taken for Yann Chevillard. I said to him: "It's weird how you look like a bloke I used to know." But I didn't tell him that the bloke

in question, he was the biggest tube that ever walked the earth. Serious. Then I took the bottle, telling them I'd be back straight away. I shot along to the living room with the idea of giving Mathilde a glass. She was still in the same place. By the window. I sat next to her. Stressed, obviously. I offered her some champers. She held out her glass. Then she said thank you. And we couldn't find anything more to say.

We stayed like that in silence for quite a while. I made out I was looking in another direction. Or reading the label on the bottle. A few people were still dancing, despite the music being turned right down. You wondered whether they were really enjoying themselves or whether they were just posing. My opinion on the matter is they were just posing. People love making you think they're enjoying themselves. They enjoy that.

Several minutes dragged by, while in my mind thousands of words were jostling around everywhere, trying to work out what to say. Then the moment came, and I leapt in with both feet.

"The music, it's not bad is it?"

"You think? I don't much like it, me."

"Yeah, that's true mind you, it's not brilliant this music … It's the kind of thing they play on the radio … "

I let it go for a moment, unsure even whether to add: "You're right frankly, it's useless this music. I haven't really been listening. It's crazy." But I thought it best to change the subject, so I wouldn't seem like a guy who's easily influenced.

"And anyway, as for atmosphere … "

"What?"

"No, I'm saying, as for atmosphere … "

" … "

I looked round.

"You get the impression they're just pretending to enjoy themselves."

"Who?"

"Ouf ... them!" I replied, pointing at two people who were dancing right in front of us.

"You think?"

"I don't really know."

She gave me a fantastic look with her green eyes. Oh my God ... I had the feeling I was just talking rubbish. But I didn't know what else to say. So I had another sip of champagne. Generally, with girls, I managed pretty well. By that I mean I didn't beat about the bush for hours. I played the seductive game and sometimes it worked. Which doesn't mean I got very far every time. It depended on the girl. And anyway, with some girls it's impossible to get far. Even if you're perfect, funny and everything, with a sense of poetry, some of them shut you out on principle, and from the way I see it that's really unpleasant. But then with Mathilde, it was different. My idea wasn't just to chat her up. Because I can tell you now that with Mathilde, me, I'd reached the point of being in love with her.

"Lucky we haven't got school tomorrow ... " I went on, so the silence didn't last too long.

"Yeah."

"We'd have died ... "

"Hm."

It's true that silence, when it lasts too long, it gets uncomfortable: you get the impression that everyone can hear what's going on in your mind.

"So here, if I've got it right, this is your father's place."

"Yeah. Well, him and his girlfriend."

"Oh, he's got a girlfriend?"

And she told me her father lived with a really young girl. Not as young as us, obviously. But even so. The way I see it, it must have been strange. But her, she didn't mention that. The only thing that bothered her was that she didn't get on with her at all. Okay, but she didn't much care. She came over to her father's as little as possible. Sometimes at the weekend, that was all. Then I asked her what it actually was, a 'teachers' training day'. She screwed up her mouth to show she was surprised at the way I kept changing the subject. It's true that my questions weren't the least bit connected. The reason was, I was always thinking about the next one while she was replying. So obviously I didn't quite catch what she said. At that moment, I don't know why, I started thinking about my mother. Yet that wasn't connected either. In my mind, I was saying that even if it hadn't been a teachers' training day, I wouldn't have been able to go to school the next day. For reasons of strategy. Because my mother, if I'd gone, she'd have found me straight away. Going to school the morning after running away, that was sticking your head in the lion's mouth. And then, you might just say that on Monday morning I'd be up for *Black Rocks*. So I couldn't go back again. Not Saturday or Monday. Not ever. It would be like putting on handcuffs and giving yourself up to the police. I began to realise there were actually lots of places that I'd have to steer clear of now. Okay. But all that, it was what was in my mind. I'd have to keep it to myself. Like a precious possession. Instead of blurting everything out to her like a burst rubber ring.

"Me, anyway, I think I'm going to take a whole week of teachers' training days."

She laughed. That made me happy. A sense of humour in a girl, it could pay dividends.

"What do you mean?" she asked me eventually.

"Ouf, that I probably won't be going to school. Not even on Monday."

"Oh?"

"Yeah."

"Why?"

"I've had some problems with my mother. It could be that I'll leave the *Institute.*"

Her expression suddenly changed.

"Is that true?"

"Yeah. Maybe."

"Really? But what happened, with your mother?"

"It's hard to explain. Let's say we've never got on very well, her and me. So maybe I'll have to go and live somewhere else."

Her eyes widened. Because usually she kept them half-closed. But now she really opened them. I sensed it interested her as a subject.

"With your father?" she asked.

"No. I can't, he's dead."

It was the first time I'd said it like that. When it came to that question, as a rule I managed to dodge it. Don't ask me why. But now, perhaps because of the drink and what I felt about her, I told her everything.

"Was it a long time ago?"

"When I was nine. He had cancer."

She looked at me without answering. In fact that whole period, it was quite hazy in my mind. To start with because I was young, after all. But also because I didn't often think about it. All I know is that my parents had split up because they never stopped arguing. Then after that, all of a sudden, he got ill, my father. It happened really quickly. We didn't even have time to get things sorted out. The memories I

have of that time, just before his illness, are that I went to stay with him every weekend. He'd rented an apartment in the same neighbourhood as us. I went to see him and I slept on the sofa bed in the living room. I can remember it well, even if it was five years ago. In the evening we often watched a video. His TV was even bigger than the one at home. But other than that, I don't really know now what we did together. Him, he looked really depressed due to not living with my mother any more. Because he must have probably still loved her. One time I even saw him crying. That just goes to show. It gave me a shock. A father, he should never cry, not to my mind. But okay, it couldn't be helped, he was too unhappy. They didn't get on, my parents. It was non-stop yelling between them. I swear to you. So it was better if they each lived in their own apartment. Even if it made him sad, my father. But that's when he got ill. Just after their break-up. I'd say: six months afterwards, something like that. After that it went like a flash. And that brought us straight to the day of his funeral, when strangely the weather was really good. My mother wore dark glasses.

That's about all I know.

"And you, your parents?" I asked her, so as not to hog the limelight.

She told me they'd been divorced for quite a while, but she thought that was just as well. The worst thing, according to her, was people who argued for years without ever having the courage to split up. In a way I agreed with her. But in my view it wasn't terribly common. Her sister, she got on better with their father. Seeing he worked in film too. He was a producer. That's the reason Émilie had been able to make her first film. You could understand the why more than the how. But her, Mathilde, she was

closer to her mother. Anyway, she told me all about herself. It really interested me. But in the end she could have spouted any old uninteresting stuff and I'd still have been mega-happy. Then she asked me what I wanted to do. "In life?" I replied. I found it odd for a girl to ask what you wanted to do in life. I thought maybe it was a bad sign. Like we didn't have much to say to each other. When you don't have much to say to each other, there's still the kind of subjects that work for everyone. But okay, I made out nothing was wrong. Nowadays the job everyone wants to do, I don't know if you've noticed, is an actor or a singer. I told her that me, I'd rather be a writer. But the moment I admitted it I felt like an idiot. And pretentious. Although it was the truth. For once I wasn't saying just any old thing. Okay. But it's not the sort of thing you say. It's showing off. So then she asked me what I wrote. And so as not to make things any easier for myself, I replied: "A novel."

"Have you got a title?"

It churned round in my head for a split second. I said the first thing that came into my mind.

"Yeah. *La Mort à Denise*," I replied. "But it's only provisional."

So then I had to explain that Denise Morozvitch, she used to be my old neighbour, and almost my grandmother, you see. We'd spent quite a lot of time together until her son shipped her off to an old people's home. That was what it talked about, my story. And while I was giving her my spiel, I thought it was a really great idea. Mathilde repeated the title out loud, as if to assess it: "*La Mort à Denise*." I was afraid of what she was going to say. Maybe that it was a crap title, in her view. Or I don't know. At any rate, to evade the issue, I decided to change the subject as soon as possible.

"So you know Marco well then," I said.

"Yeah."

That froze me out. She said it as if it was obvious.

"How come?"

"Ouf, I don't know. He's a friend of my sister's. They were in the same class, ages ago. And we live nearby. Two streets away from one another. That's why. But I don't know him well."

As we were talking, most people were getting ready to leave. You couldn't tell whether they were going home or on to the famous nightclub. Just the end of a party, like. Besides, we'd finished our drinks. And the bottle I'd fetched was empty. Not because we'd been drinking like mad, but because it was already virtually empty when I got it. She was thirsty. I told her that the drink was to be found in the bathroom. We got up. And we went down the corridor. But there was just the dark-haired girl in the bathroom now, smoking her superior quality cigarette. She asked me where Marco was. I said I didn't know. "You can tell him I'm waiting for him in here," she added. That made Mathilde laugh a fantastic little laugh. Then, as we went past her room, she beckoned to me: "Come and see." She wanted to show me something apparently. I followed her without a word. I swear to you. Into her room, where she slept and everything. Okay. She closed the door after her. I couldn't get over it. And that's where I discovered something that knocked me flat.

4

HER ROOM was normal except for the walls, which were covered in posters of horses. I'm not joking. Like Bénédicte, like. She looked at a sort of clock above her desk. It was almost two o'clock.

"You ride?" I asked, not batting an eyelid, despite feeling awkward and surprised.

"Yes. Every week."

"Oh? That's … cool."

"I love it."

Okay. I admit I'd changed my tune a bit.

"Me too."

"You too?"

"Yes. Horses, they're my pet subject."

I imagined Bénédicte hearing me say that. Fuck. It would have given her something to take the piss out of me for. Seeing that "horses, they're my pet subject", was what I said all the time to take the piss out of her. It usually sent her into a rage. She chased me round the apartment with her riding crop, trying to hit me. Which goes to show how strange life can be.

"Where do you do it?"

The name of my future stepsister's club, I couldn't remember it now. I preferred being evasive.

"I mostly do it in the holidays actually. I've an uncle who lives near Nice. He's got a field."

"Oh?"

"Yeah. For grazing, it's convenient."

The truth was I'd never even tried to get on a horse's back.

"And you?" I went on.

"Every Saturday. In Boulogne."

"Boulogne, that's convenient too … compared with Nice."

I admired her posters again. She must have realised that I thought it was odd for a girl to put up that sort of thing. Anyway, as if to explain herself she told me what I knew already: namely, that this wasn't really her room. Seeing that during the week she lived somewhere else. She came to her father's as little as possible. And so her room in this apartment, she'd never really decorated it. But I was still relieved.

It was then she beckoned to me again. Beckoning was obviously her thing. I went over to her. She opened the window.

"Look."

The view was incredible. Because of how high we were. On one side was the Eiffel Tower, which was already in darkness. A bit further to the left, the Musée d'Orsay. And the Seine, winding away into the distance. And everything plunged in deepest sleep. It was mind-blowing to have this view from your bedroom. All to yourself.

"It's stunning," I remarked.

Then I noticed the window opposite. Because it was the only one where there was still a light on. Mathilde smiled, to say that that was what she'd actually wanted to show me. Just that: this window in the middle of the night. A smile was enough. It intrigued me. Because of the light it was like a window opening onto another world. It could have been a library. Or an office. Whatever, but there was a wooden table and quite a lot of books everywhere. And a globe as well.

"The light's always on in that window at night."

"Why?"

"I don't know, actually. I wonder … It's on every night, but there's never anyone there."

"It's strange … "

"It's something I'd love to know … "

We stayed for a long time, gazing at it. Wondering what might happen in that room at night. It was like an enigma. A few yards away from us, despite the gap and the six floors. You had the impression that you could have reached out your hand and almost touched it, this office. It was nice. We were side by side, our shoulders were just touching, and it was as silent as a church. There was a slight breeze which ruffled her hair. I could hear her breathing. Just there. And yet I wasn't there, at her bedroom window: I was across the street. In the deserted office. And I told myself it must be a writer's study, and that was probably why she'd wanted to show me. Since I'd told her I wanted to be one, a writer. Then I thought that she must often look at it, this office. Maybe every night before going to sleep. When she was staying with her father. And every time she wondered why there was a light, although it was empty. Every night, the same mystery. With her hair in the breeze. Yeah, that was it, what I was thinking. And I imagined her at her window. Dreamy and everything, Mathilde. And I was really overcome that she'd asked me to look with her, just for tonight. And that we should both have wondered, without even saying, why the light was on in that office when no one seemed to write in there. Words, they were pointless now. There was nothing to say, except that it was wonderful. But even that, there was no need to tell each other. Because we understood one another. The sight spoke for itself. And us, all we had to do now was be silent in the

face of this mystery. Like whenever something important happens. Yes, I was overcome. I shivered at her bedroom window. Because I knew what she'd asked me to look at with her was something really rare and precious. And that nothing could spoil the power of this moment. Nothing. That's what I thought. The world, at that moment, it could collapse. I'm not joking. It could disappear. I was ready. Besides, everything will disappear one day. Everything will change. There's nothing we can do about it, that's the way it is. But there's one thing that'll never change, I thought. One thing that'll withstand the destruction of the world. And that's the joy of having been close to her. At this precise spot. At this precise moment.

Mathilde, she was really an exceptional girl. If I'd dared that's what I'd have told her, but I didn't dare, so I said nothing. But even if I'd dared I wouldn't have had the time anyway, since someone knocked at the door. She looked at me as if we were to say our goodbyes. I was really touched by that. Then she opened the door. It was Marco from Morocco. And behind him the dark-haired girl with her nipples sticking out.

"Ah, there you both are!" What are you doing?" he asked Mathilde.

"What? Nothing."

Then, after glancing in my direction, she added: "We were talking."

"Well? We're the last ones here … they've all gone already!"

Mathilde said she wasn't going to come with us. In fact I'd noticed she didn't much like them, her sister's friends. I'd have loved to stay with her, me, but no one suggested it. I had no idea what I was expecting to do. In a way I preferred not to end up by myself. But in another I was

afraid I wouldn't be able to get into this nightclub of theirs. And once I was there I knew I'd be bored out of my mind. Seeing I never dance. As a rule, from what Marco started to say, the district was teeming with nightclubs. There was no need to go to Timbuktu. You only had to walk a few yards.

But Émilie absolutely had to go to some place near Bastille. Don't ask me why. So basically we were supposed to get a taxi. Even several taxis. Seeing there were quite a few of us.

"Right. We'd better go then … "

Marco turned to Mathilde to give her a kiss. At that moment we heard a really deep voice in the corridor. It was her father. We came out of her room, putting on our best behaviour. She introduced everyone. He was an impressive-looking guy. With jet black hair. He didn't look in a very good mood or anything. We got the message that it was time to push off. Mathilde showed us to the door.

"Okay then, bye," I said.

"Bye … "

She was rather cool on account of Marco being there, and the other girl who was called Alice. She just gave a little smile. I was really torn, as I didn't know when I was going to be able to see her again. But at the same time I was fine. Because that moment we'd spent together, at her window, it was a really great moment.

Still, I added, "See you soon."

She opened the door. Just then Marco realised he'd left his jacket behind. He went rushing off to the furthest bedroom. Straightway I told myself he was going to run into Mathilde's father, and he'd be ultra-embarrassed. Us, we stayed there by the door, not saying anything in particular. It put me under pressure. Several times I thought

of going up to her to kiss her, but that scared the hell out of me, even if I thought it was stupid to be scared of a kiss. But it was because of Alice. It made me feel edgy. To kiss a girl you need to have certain conditions. I told myself: I'll count to three and then I'll do it. But when I got to three I went back to nought. Anyway. I let the opportunity slip, and Marco reappeared.

"You're sure you don't want to come?"

"Yeah yeah."

"Too bad. Right, bye."

Marco gave her a kiss. Then Alice did. Then me. And our lips, at the spot they call the corner of the mouth, they touched slightly. Just slightly. It stunned me. But I didn't know if I was dreaming or what. Or whether it meant something. Anyway, at the time I really believed it did. Not a kiss. No. But almost. She gave a funny smile. And the door closed behind us. I didn't know what to think any more, other than that I was happy. At least I think I was.

5

É MILIE'S CROWD were supposed to be waiting for us in the street. Except that when we got out into the rue Pierre-Charron there was no one there. They'd all cleared off already. Marco started going wild. It rather got to him that we were both witnesses to it, me and Alice. My opinion is that he was so proud, the slightest little hitch was enough to drive him mad. He got out his mobile, saying he'd get everything sorted. He got their voicemail. That was a foregone conclusion. So he tried some other numbers. No joy. They'd had a bit too much to drink, the others, they'd blown us away completely, and we ended up like twats out on the street. The bum option, like. Me, I didn't take much notice of all that. I was trying to see the Fermat's windows, but it wasn't actually possible from where we were, as their apartment looked onto the inner courtyard. From what I could make out, Alice was a childhood friend of Émilie's. They knew each other well. But when she rang, she got her voicemail too. So I suggested going for a drink. It wasn't the greatest of ideas. Okay, but we hadn't got anything better to do. Both of them left messages. They thought they'd ring us back quickly. While we waited, there was no point staying outside. What I was dreading most of all, me, was that they'd both go home and I'd be left on my own. We hotfooted it towards the Champs. And the thing was we didn't see anyone. Not even at the taxi rank. Marco, you could tell he was really rather disgusted. Because if the truth be known, I'm sure of it, he was wondering whether they'd

done it on purpose to get shot of us. From my point of view it was so much the better. I'd no desire to spend the night with schmucks. That's why I started slagging them off a bit. To console Marco. After three minutes he thought the same as I did: Émilie's crowd, they were a real load of saddos. Even the girls.

We went back up the avenue a way towards the Arc de Triomphe. "Wait for me," Alice kept shouting, following us despite her high heels. We had to keep waiting for her. Then I told Marco I'd got to draw out some cash. I went to a cashpoint and got a straight thousand euros. I swear to you. That was the most it could cough up, the machine. Otherwise I'd have got ten thousand. I put the wad in my inside jacket pocket. That did something for me. A bit like my first communion. Then I told Marco that it was okay, we could go. He didn't see anything, him. Too busy staring at Alice's cleavage. I was really pleased with my stunt. The look he'd have on his face when I showed him all that.

But at the same time I was stressed out. It was a bit dodgy, the Champs. At that time of night it was crawling with riffraff. What's more, Marco began telling us this unbelievable story. I swear to you. About how a friend of his mother's had tried to draw out some money on the Champs in the middle of the night, actually. And then he'd felt the cold barrel of a gun in the back of his neck. I swear to you. Really, a gun in the back of his neck. This wasn't Paraguay! In France, I tell you! And some bloke asked him to get into his motor, which was parked on the side of the road. There was nothing he could do, this friend of Marco's mother. He had to get in the motor or else he might have had his brains blown out. In short, he found himself in a pretty crap situation. With a tooled-up lunatic who was really freaking out, who was driving flat out and who told

him to shut it whenever he tried to ask where he was taking him. The bloke with the shooter, he didn't want to hear the sound of Marco's mother's friend's voice. He told him if he heard it again, his voice, it'd be for the last time, because he'd do him in as soon as look at him. And so he didn't hear it for the rest of the journey, although it lasted for over half-an-hour. Direction—the suburbs. The other bloke, the one with the shooter, he couldn't have been in a right frame of mind, according to Marco. Because he was hyper worked up and everything. Anyway, after a terrible half-hour he told him to get out of the car. They'd arrived. It was a kind of waste ground. In the middle of nowhere. Basically. He really thought he was going to be bumped off, the friend of Marco's mother. Otherwise why would he have been brought to this waste ground? He begged, but the other guy wouldn't listen. He told him to get on his knees, in the middle of the open ground, hands on his head, and to stop blubbing like a girl. They were waiting for someone. That's what the bloke with the gun told him. They were waiting for two of his mates. To do what? Nobody knew. But doubtless nothing nice.

They waited. But the two characters, the ones they were waiting for, they didn't show up. So the bloke with the shooter, it got him even more worked up, waiting like that in the cold for some guys who weren't coming. He was talking to himself, saying incomprehensible things. A crazy, like. And freaking out. Marco's mother's friend was shaking, he was afraid he was going to piss himself. He said his prayers. It went on for at least half-an-hour. Full-on torture. But in the end the bloke told him to get up and clear off. "Go on, disappear," he said. The truth is he'd had enough of waiting, he realised his mates weren't coming. He didn't even take his wallet, the bloke. Which

shows he hadn't done it for the money. But for what, then? He always asked himself that afterwards, Marco's mother's friend. But now he's quite happy not to know the answer. There are things you'd rather not know for the rest of your life. Still, it sends a shiver down your spine to think about it.

"Why are you telling us this?" I said, walking a bit faster, although discreetly.

"No reason."

No reason. That killed me.

After thirty yards or so we turned right, into a little street where there were still lights on. There was a sort of bar here that Marco knew. Or so he said. It was one of the only places in the area that was still open. Or we'd have had to go to a nightclub, but the two of us, and Marco, we weren't too keen on that. We preferred to just find a table and have a drink together. When we opened the door the music hit you in the face. We sat at a table. The atmosphere was pretty good. A girl came straight over to us. I swear to you. But it was a waitress. Marco wanted beers. Small time, like. So I cut him short, sort of self-assured and everything, and said: "Champagne!"

"Three glasses?" she asked, to get things quite clear.

I immediately put her straight:

"No no. A bottle!"

She looked surprised. Marco too.

"It's on me," I explained.

The girl waited to see what Marco would say, as if everything depended on his opinion and that it was him who decided. A silly bitch. Then he said okay, and at last she left us alone. Waitresses, most of the time they're silly

bitches. They don't know anything about life, on account of serving drinks to all and sundry. Especially since beer, it's okay when you're fourteen. But after that it doesn't do much for you. You have to go on to something else. Champagne, that's cool. Which is what I said to Marco: "Champagne, that's cool!" But he didn't hear. You couldn't talk because of the music. If you wanted to say something you had to shout. So I shouted again: "It's better to stay with champagne!"

I looked round. Virtually no girls. Just blokes. Most of them, you wondered where on earth they came from. Dressed like nerds and everything. The type who drink beer, if you see what I mean. A middle-of-the-road sort of place, basically. And Alice especially, you got the impression she was wondering what the hell she was doing here, frankly. With us two. She looked round with a stunned expression. Yet when I think back on everything that happened afterwards, I tell myself it was still a good moment in that bar. It's afterwards that things went wrong.

The girl brought us the bottle in front of everyone. This way for the international class. Even so she still asked me to pay straight away, so we wouldn't do a runner, which must happen sometimes. But me, it didn't bother me to pay straight away, seeing that's all I'd been waiting for for the last ten minutes: to pay right under Marco's nose. So I got out a hundred euro note, straight off, but she took it without turning a hair, everyday event sort of thing, so to impress her I added:

"Keep the change."

Like in the films, like. I couldn't get over it. Nor could Marco. He thought he was seeing things. In fact we both thought we were seeing things. It definitely impressed us. At that moment Alice got up to go to the toilet, and it was

just the two of us. Man to man. Marco still hadn't moved on from the business with the tip. Then, so he'd realise that a little thing like that wasn't going to stop me, I showed him my wad of cash, but mega-discreetly. It knocked him dead.

"Fuck. Where did you get all that?"

"In Morocco," I replied, to annoy him.

I have to say I was on top form just then. Because of Mathilde. Even if I couldn't work out if I'd got all het up over the business of the kiss or not. Sometimes there are things, you don't know whether they really happened or whether you made them up. Okay, but what was certain was that I felt something strong inside me.

"So? What do you think of her?"

"Mathilde?" I asked.

"No! Alice."

"Don't know."

"The problem is, you see, she's already got a bloke. And it seems she's still fond of him … I spent the evening trying things but … "

I wasn't listening at all. I was elsewhere. I was thinking about the thing with the kiss again. In fact I think our lips hadn't really touched. But almost.

"Aren't you listening to me any more? What are you thinking about?"

Marco began to get unpleasant. You could bet it was because he was offended at having been knocked back by the others. And also by Alice, who apparently didn't want to kiss him. And now it was my turn to gently knock him back by being deaf to what he was saying. Like a singer that no one listens to any more. Marco, he was the sort who always needs to be at the centre of the conversation. That sort, me, they do me in. But it was him who was getting

more aggressive than ever, when it should have been me. He went back over my thing with Charlotte again. The girl I'd made him think I had a date with. According to him I was talking rubbish. And then he started on about Mathilde, and that was distinctly unfunny. Seeing they'd caught us, her and me, talking in her room, he started getting worked up. But most of all, from what he said, you got the impression he'd been out with her already and that he was quite happy to leave her to me, since she was only knee-high to a grasshopper anyway. I couldn't get over it.

"It's you who's talking rubbish," I counter-attacked. "She's not my type at all, Mathilde."

The thing is, I didn't want him interfering with all that.

"Oh yeah?"

"Yeah. Not at all."

"And what is your type?"

"My type of girl?"

"Yeah. What is your type of girl?"

I looked round to find an example. But there were just blokes apart from the waitress, and she was a bitch. I shrugged. Marco kept laughing to take the piss out of me, and that drove me nuts. So I poured two more glasses of champagne, just to buy myself some time to think of an answer. Then I asked to see his mobile. To begin with it was just to keep him quiet. I never really anticipated what was going to happen. He gave it to me with an amused look, not understanding, and I showed him the number on the screen, the last call he'd received, and said:

"See that, it's the phone number of my type of girl … "

"Oh yeah?"

He didn't believe me. So I brought up the big guns:

"You know her, anyway. Actually you know her very well."

"So who is it?"

"Madame Thomas."

It took a while for him to get what I meant.

"Sure," he eventually replied.

"I'm telling you."

"Come off it … "

"I was with her when I called you just now. Before coming to join you … "

"Do you take me for an fool or what?"

"That's her first name, Madame Thomas. Charlotte. She's called Charlotte Thomas."

His face! Marco and me, we'd often talked about her, Madame Thomas. According to him she was the sublime of sublimes.

"You expect me to believe that this Charlotte you were talking about just now, the one you so-called dumped, is the French teacher?"

"I didn't want to tell you at first, but okay, now you've got her number on your phone, I'm going to have to let you in on it."

"Rubbish … "

"But promise me you'll never repeat it to anyone."

"Repeat what? That you're sleeping with your teacher?"

"It's mega-important that you're discreet, seeing she's married and that her and me, you see, it's an absolute total secret."

My tongue was running away with me.

"Yeah yeah … "

"Especially as she might be pregnant … "

He started laughing again, as if I was pulling his chain. At the time it annoyed me. When for once I was telling the truth.

"You don't believe me?"

"No."

"You don't believe me?"

"I've just told you I don't."

I thought for a second. Just then Alice came back from the bog. She finished her drink, giving us a funny look as if she was trying to work out what we were talking about. But at the same time she didn't much care.

"Okay. Go on then," I went on, "call that number. Then you'll see who you get."

"Get away … "

"Go on, I'm telling you … All you have to do is ask to speak to Julien Parme. She'll understand. Seeing I made a call from her mobile just now. You'll see … "

"But it's really late … "

"You see, you're losing it … "

"No I'm not … "

He glanced at Alice, who shrugged because she didn't understand, unless it was a kind of challenge. She must have thought we were ten-year-olds. So Marco pressed recall. Suddenly he looked nervous. The truth is, he wasn't feeling so clever now. But he hadn't seen anything yet. That gave me a thrill.

"It's ringing … "

"'Course it's ringing … "

We waited for a moment.

"Who is it you're calling?" asked Alice.

But we were so preoccupied that we didn't answer.

"Ah. It's their voicemail … " he said, relieved at his discovery.

He listened to the outgoing message. Suddenly he went pale. He'd just realised who it belonged to, this voicemail: Madame Thomas.

"Fuck, it's her … "

He couldn't get over it, the guy.

"Course it's her."

"Who?" Alice asked again.

He was in a daze for at least ten seconds, and then he went on.

"But what were you doing?"

"What do you think … "

I looked up at the ceiling, as if it was obvious.

"When you called me, you were with her?"

"Yeah. We were at her place. In her bedroom, if you want the details. Afterwards I wanted to come and see you all. Okay, but the party, just between you and me, you rather over-hyped it. It's not bad this champagne, is it?"

You should have seen his face.

"I don't believe it … "

"What are you two talking about?"

"It's totally crazy, basically. He's having it away with one of our teachers … I just got her on the phone. I don't believe it … He's having it away with the French teacher!"

I didn't say another word. I left him like that, gobsmacked, a dwarf in the presence of the Unbelievable, and got up and went for a piss too. He sat there alone with Alice, reduced to rubble.

I'd got my revenge.

When I came back, Marco was still where I'd left him. He was staring into space. Alice was making conversation but I could see he wasn't listening. What's more, I'd hardly sat down before he started bombarding me with questions. How had I managed it? What was she like in bed? How long had it been going on? He wanted to know everything, basically. But I was deliberately evasive. Just to drive him mad.

"So who is she, this teacher?" asked Alice.

Then the time came for the bar to close. I didn't know they closed so early, me, bars. It must have been about three in the morning. Maybe even four. And the others still hadn't rung back. Too bad. Still, we weren't about to beg them. But what quite annoyed me was the thought that the bar was closing already. I'd have liked to keep going till early morning. But no. It wasn't possible. The place gradually emptied like a bath, and we found ourselves naked with no water: as far as atmosphere went, it sucked. We got the message that it was time to leave. And that's how we wound up in the street.

"Right. Where are you going?" Marco asked, yawning. The million-dollar question.

"And you? Are you getting a cab?"

"Don't know … "

"I am. I'll drop you off if you like."

Knight in shining armour, like. But above all I didn't much want to end up on my own in this neighbourhood. The story he'd told me about the bloke with the gun wasn't the kind of thing to make me feel safe. Fear of violence, it exists. Ever since I'd got my cash from the cashpoint I'd had the instincts of a rich man. At the next election I'd have almost voted right-wing, if I'd been old enough. Which would have been really significant actually, seeing I'm usually more for the other side, I mean: for equality; and the worst type of inequality, to my mind, is that it's always those who most need money who have the least of it.

We didn't have too long to wait. On the Champs, a taxi straightway pulled up in front of us. A second later the three of us were driving through the darkened streets of Paris. Marco, he didn't say another word. I wasn't sure if it was because he was knackered. Or whether he was disgusted.

But in my opinion what was on his mind was me and Madame Thomas. So he totally ignored Alice. Me, I was dreading the moment we arrived outside his place. Then I wouldn't know what to do. A shudder ran right through me. I checked my stash was safe: I'd still got about ten fags left. In fact I hadn't smoked much all evening. Okay. I'd always have that to do: smoke. It's not true that the dog is man's best friend. Man's best friend is the cigarette. Okay, but I wasn't about to spend the rest of the night chain-smoking. What else could I do? I couldn't work it out. My mind was swimming all over the place. When I shut my eyes it made my head spin. I'd had too much to drink.

In the meantime Alice was talking to herself. It must have made an ultra-bad end to her evening being with us two, but she looked as if she was in a good mood. Alice, she was the sort of girl who was always in a good mood. A nice girl, at the end of the day. Anyway. We arrived outside Marco's place. Back where we started. He shook my hand. "I've got to talk to you tomorrow … " "I'll call you," I said. Then I added: "Watch out you don't make too much noise on your way in. Remember your grandmother … " I was just kidding him. But I could tell from his face that the blow had struck home. Because him, he was forever trying to make us think he lived on his own, sort of like a student. He never told the truth anyway, Marco. Never. Alice got out of the taxi. I wondered what would happen. They kissed each other there on the street, sort of coolly, normal and everything, and then she sat back down beside me. I thought it was odd. We saw Marco disappear through his door. It really hadn't been his evening. But that couldn't be helped. Everyone has their good and bad days. Alice gave me a little smile. Me, despite a bad start, I'd had rather a good day. Even though it had been night for a long time already.

6

THE NEXT THING was that I had to straightway answer the driver's question, namely: "Where am I dropping you next?" I always find it odd, me, when someone calls me '*vous*', don't you? Sometimes it takes a real time before I work out it's me they're talking to. Okay, but here you couldn't be too sure: it might have been her or both of us that he was talking to. "Where are you going?" I asked her. She gave the driver her address. Then she added, for my benefit: "It's by the Eiffel Tower." It suited me fine that she replied so quickly. Because me, I didn't know exactly where I was going. But maybe I'd have said the same thing if the driver had asked me where he could drop me: "At the Eiffel Tower." It would have been a bit stupid, seeing there's zilch to do round there. Especially in the middle of the night. Okay, but at the same time I wouldn't have had any better ideas. In fact Paris, to be honest, I didn't know a whole lot of it—even though I've lived here all my life. Besides, most people who live in Paris, nine times out of ten they don't know it well. I'm not joking. And if you ask them where you can drop them, when they haven't had a chance to think about it, nine times out of ten they'll reply instinctively: "At the Eiffel Tower." I think that's mad.

What was mad too, was that to get there we went down my street. It gave me a peculiar sensation. I nearly said something to Alice, but she wouldn't have understood why I didn't get out if it was where I lived. Out of the window I tried to see if the lights were still on in the living room. I couldn't really see: the taxi was going too fast. And

besides, I preferred to discreetly eye up Alice's breasts, whose nipples were still sticking out. I wondered how they managed it, the pair of them. Never tired. Right. But then I got the feeling she'd caught me at it. Anyway, she said:

"So you, this thing with your teacher, it's true then?"

I didn't know what to say. So I thought it best to cut to the chase.

"Yes. Why? But it's complicated. She's too much in love. Whereas for me, you see, she's more of a friend … "

"But how old is she?"

"About thirty."

I couldn't get over it. It even impressed me, that. I'd have given anything for it to be true.

"It must be strange," she remarked, thoughtfully.

"These days, you know, it's no big deal any more, the age difference. Look at Émilie Fermat's father's girlfriend. She's twenty."

"Get away … "

"I swear to you."

Okay. But while we were chatting, I couldn't keep my eyes off her breasts. It was crazy: they had a magnetic effect on me. Even if I tried to look at her eyes or out the window, I automatically came back to them. Sometimes I got the impression they were talking to me or sending me signals: "Julien, yoo-hoo, we're here … " It drove me completely nuts. At that moment I'd have liked to marry them. And to start something serious. Have a house and everything. And a car with lots of little breasts in the back. In a word, it drove me nuts.

It reminded me of a strip cartoon, I can't remember what it's called now, which my local bookshop had had in the window not so long ago. The cover was actually of a girl opening her blouse like an offering. You could

see her breasts. Right there on the cover. It's one of the most beautiful things I've seen in my life. So of course I'd gone into the bookshop, and I'd started flicking through it, this strip cartoon. I'd found the part in the story where she bares her breasts. It was two lovers running through a forest because they were being chased by someone or other. Then they managed to find a hiding place somewhere in the bushes. That's when the guy said to her: "Show them to me one last time." And the girl undid her blouse, slowly, and then she pushed him away and closed her eyes. So he could see. It was really beautiful, I swear to you. A woman who does that. For no reason. Just out of generosity. At the time I always made a little detour on my way back from school so I could go past the window. Like an important appointment. What made me laugh was that there were always one or two little old men outside, pretending to look at the novels in the window. Perverts, you could bet on it.

Several times I was unsure whether to kiss her or not, Alice. But we were already not far from the Eiffel Tower. And more than anything my mind was on Mathilde. I thought again about the time I'd spent with her in her room. And about the story of the office that was lit up all night. So I turned to Alice and asked her what she thought about it.

"Imagine an office, on the sixth floor of a building sort of thing … "

"Yeah … "

"Okay. Now imagine that every night there's a light on in it, this office. As if there was someone who worked there instead of sleeping, you see … "

"Yeah … "

149

"Okay. But imagine, too, that there's never anyone in this office."

"Yeah … "

"No one, you understand … it's permanently empty. Every night."

"And?"

"What does it mean, do you think? Why's there a light on in this office every night if no one works there?"

She thought for a moment. Then as the taxi pulled up at the kerb so she could get out, she said:

"You got any more questions like that?"

She didn't see the poetry of the thing. It must have been obvious that I was expecting a proper reply. Then she added: "I don't know. Perhaps the guy who works there always forgets to switch the light off when he leaves … " Not a bad suggestion. Even if in my view that wasn't it. Then she gave me a kiss. We said see you soon. But as I kissed her I don't know what got into me, but I put my hand on her left breast, the one by her heart. I swear to you. She stood stock still, but without any attempt to move away. On the contrary. So I stroked it again. Like a madman who's got three minutes to seize hold of the beauty of the world. Then I asked: "You're going in then?" She just said yes. As if it was obvious. All the time smiling. She opened the main door. The thing is, I ought to have got out with her. Even if she didn't let me go up to her place. Just to try. But I didn't dare. I watched her disappear behind the door of her building.

"What shall we do now" I asked the driver.

"Ouf, I don't know. That's up to you."

"To the Gare Montparnasse, then," I replied, without knowing why there and not somewhere else.

I was burning up inside so much because of Alice's breasts that I came close to telling the driver that on second thoughts I wanted to go back to the Porte Dauphine. Where I'd seen those girls earlier in the evening. Just to get free from these intrusive thoughts. But in the end, the idea of the station, it was a good one. Because trains start running very early. I thought: 'In less than two hours, life will be back to normal. It won't kill me to wait two hours … ' I'd done worse already. Especially since at a station most of the cafés must have opened at dawn. I checked on the dashboard of the taxi. Just after four o'clock in the morning. Out of the window I watched the empty streets go by. On the radio they were playing: *Que reste-t-il de nos amours?* Things were fine. I told myself that this morning I'd call Madame Thomas and tell her it was over between us. I'd met another woman. She was called Mathilde. And I wanted to marry her. I was crazy, basically. And the music went on, melancholy and everything. Things were fine. I could have stayed in the taxi for two hours, going round and round the city. Half asleep from drink. Or I could have asked him how much it would cost to go to the sea. Normandy, for instance, that was about two hours. I'd arrive almost as the sun was coming up. That would be fine too. I'd let myself be soothed by the music all the way. I'd got the money for it. And then I'd walk along the beach. Before having breakfast in an ultra-smart hotel. Then I'd send a message to Alice's breasts to tell them to come quickly and join me in the room I'd booked with a view of the sea. But I daren't ask the driver. He'd have given me a funny look, the bloke. Especially as it wouldn't have been difficult to work out that I'd run away from home. And then you couldn't predict how he'd react.

I closed my eyes slightly to imagine the sea. Which shows I was beginning to feel tired. In fact the kind of seaside I

liked best, it wasn't Normandy but Brittany. With seagulls and everything. Because once, my father used to take me there every summer. I don't remember much about what we did there any more. I can picture it of course, but it's a bit hazy now. Like everything connected with my father. What I'd really like, sometimes, is to have an exact memory of everything I've done so far in life. Even at my age, that would be quite a lot already. I'm sure it would almost be enough to make me happy. I'd be like grandmothers who spend half the day among their memories. What I realised with Madame Morozvitch is that most of the time they're happy, grandmothers. On the other side of their eyelids they've got pictures that no one else can see. Like treasures. They travel there, in their memory, cut off from the world. They bring people who've been dead for ages and ages back to life. In fact they live with them. But as I see it, to live with the dead you don't need to be a grandmother. For instance, one thing I remember is that to go to Brittany with my father, we always went from the Gare Montparnasse, and before getting on the train we always went to the newsagents where he bought hundreds of magazines, including *The Life and Times of Scrooge McDuck* for me. The driver dropped me by the station. It made me feel strange, even if it's a pathetic thing to think, to tell myself that I'd already been to this very spot with my father. Places, after all, they almost never change. Us, we rush around. But the world, when you think about it, it hardly ever changes.

I took out a fifty euro note. The driver gaped. He didn't have any change. Or so he said. I shrugged my shoulders to say he could keep the lot. I didn't care. He couldn't get over it, the bloke. I sensed he was wondering whether to say something to me, but in the end no, he didn't say anything. He just started up and drove off. In the darkness it was so

deserted you could hear the noise of his engine for over a minute. As if we were in the country, in fact. Except that we were right in the heart of Paris. I walked round the square outside for a while. It was a peculiar sort of sensation. You'd have thought it was the day after a huge disaster. In which most Parisians had been wiped out … I imagined being the last person alive. Because I'd thought to have a nuclear shelter built under my bed. I really wonder what I could have got up to. In my opinion, after a few days I'd have been too depressed. And people would have begun to miss me, except my mother of course. Okay. I went and sat on a bench. Then I lit a cigarette. Things were fine. I looked up at the Tour Montparnasse, which seemed enormous from below. But after three minutes I told myself it wasn't a good idea to stay here. I couldn't sit still. So I decided to have a look round the area. Just to kill time. It was pretty stupid to leave home just to sit on a bench doing nothing. There must have definitely been things going on in this part of town. At night-time they swarm round everywhere, but in secret. All you have to do is search a bit and open the right doors.

I thought I'd walk round the streets and just take things as they came. That's how, after at least twenty minutes of going round and round, I landed up in the rue de la Gaîté, not far from the station. It's a fantastic name, I think. I love it. Me, I'd have really liked to live at this address: 'Julien Parme, I, rue de la Gaîté'. It would be a small apartment that I'd share with Mathilde. And an extra room on the top floor for me to write in. Nobody would have permission to go into this room. There'd just be a table, a lamp and thousands of books. It'd be there, for example, where I'd have written my greatest novels. And my poetry. Just before

they died, important personalities from the arts would make a special trip to the rue de la Gaîté to meet me. And the ones who were already too far gone to be able to travel, would ask on their death bed, as a last wish: "Read me a few more lines of Parme … "

Such was the state of my daydreaming when I noticed that the rue de la Gaîté, in fact it was just crawling with porn clubs. I swear. And what's more, it was totally by chance that I'd come across this street. Sometimes I tell myself: I've really got a sixth sense. But I couldn't work out what sort of bars they were exactly. Still, it was the only place in the entire neighbourhood that looked to have any life in it. The rest had definitely taken sleeping pills. So I went over to the lights. The only ones still on at the time. And that's when I realised that these seedy places were actually closed as well. Only they left the lights on all night. Don't ask me why. But it meant I could have a good letch. As if I was in a sex museum. Okay, but the thing was, you couldn't see a whole lot. Just a few photos of naked girls, but with black tape over the interesting bits. Shame. But frankly I wondered what went on inside, if there were girls who took their clothes off and showed their breasts, and especially if you could do things with them or if it was just for looking. I thought that one idea was maybe to go up to Pigalle where, obviously, there would still be a few things open. Me, I don't know what it is that I've got about girls' breasts, but it knocks me sideways. For girls' breasts I'd be prepared to cross Paris. But I started thinking about Mathilde again, and that worked better than a cold shower. I thought: maybe she was hoping we'd kiss each other just now? Perhaps I'd disappointed her. How could I tell? In any case, girls, I don't understand them at all, me. Sometimes I understand, but it's always too late. I'm like

a blind man. Even if sometimes I try and make out that I
can see in the dark.

What there also was in this part of town was thousands of
crêperies. They must have been for the Bretons, I thought.
Before they catch their trains. Bretons eat crêpes. That's the
way it is. That too, don't ask me why. And then I saw a
shapeless mass lying on the ground. It was a kind of tramp,
and it made me uneasy walking right past him. I'd have rather
crossed the street. But I didn't have time. So as I went by I
had a good look at him. He was asleep, rolled up in a filthy
dirty sleeping bag. It upset me. Until I realised that I was
in almost the same situation. Serious. And that maybe he'd
started like me: walking in the night without knowing where
to go. It sent a shiver down my spine, thinking that. I swear
to you. Especially as just then his dog, which I hadn't seen
at first, pricked up its ears then got up and started following
me. To begin with that made me stressed. Some dogs are
really aggressive. I know a guy who got badly bitten by a
dog like that. So I walked a bit faster, but him too, he walked
faster. I didn't know what to do any more. So I stopped. He
stopped as well. Basically, he was doing the same as me. "Go
back to your master!" I whispered to him. "Go on! Off with
you! Leave me alone!" But he stood there looking at me. In
fact it wasn't hard to guess that he was nice, this mutt. In
any case he didn't look at all like the type to bite you. "Go
on, clear off … " But it was no use. He wasn't listening. So I
decided to pretend he wasn't there. And I carried on. At the
end of the street, just before the boulevard, I turned round.
He was still behind me, still with that look that said take me
with you. I didn't know what to do any more. It made me
sad for the tramp. He didn't have a whole lot as it was. And

if on top of that he woke up to find that even his dog had abandoned him ... I thought: maybe it's just because he's hungry and his master hasn't got anything more to feed him with. The worst tyrant is always the stomach. What I heard is that tramps, when they have a dog, all the money they get from begging, they spend it on their dog. I swear to you. In fact most of the time tramps are the least selfish people you can imagine. They're generous, even. Kind-hearted.

Then the dog went past me and crossed the boulevard Montparnasse without even looking. Luckily there were virtually no cars coming. There too, it was pretty much deserted. But it was still dangerous. I wasn't quite sure what he was looking for. As it was he sniffed at things every few yards. It worried me to let him flit around like that in the middle of the road, so I whistled and he straightway came to me. No fool, this dog. Got whatever he wanted. Next he was dancing round my feet as if we were on our honeymoon. What I'd have really liked was to give him something to eat, but at that time of night I didn't see what. So I carried on the way I was going, and set off along the rue de Rennes. Him too. I had the impression it was getting colder and colder. And tiredness too, I was beginning to seriously feel it. As a result the rue de Rennes seemed endless. Really endless. A street that would never come to an end. Like a conveyor belt. Or in a nightmare. However far you walk, walk, walk, you never get to the end. Then the point comes when you realise there isn't one, an end. That's a blow, obviously. So you stop exhausting yourself, you give up, and the conveyor belt takes you right back where you came from. It's often like that, life.

I can't tell you how long I walked like that. But when I turned round the dog had disappeared. He must have gone

back to his master. So much the better, I thought. Even so I was surprised just how lifeless it was in this part of town. In my mind I had the impression that amazing things happened at night while everyone was asleep. Yet now, strangely, the only impression I got was actually that yes, everyone was asleep. At the same time I told myself that it was very likely because I wasn't in the right place. What I had to do was keep walking until I found something. I couldn't even tell you what I was looking for exactly. I carried on along the embankments, through the Saint-Michel quarter. It was dead dismal. Except that then I saw a bar that was open. Actually it wasn't a bar but a 'tavern'. I swear to you, it was written over the front. Me, I thought it was just in Switzerland that they still existed, taverns. And last century, too. But no. There was one right here, by the Seine. It made me laugh. I looked in the window to see what it was like. But you couldn't see anything. Anyway, most places, you can't see what they're like from outside. That way it forces customers to come in. Cunning. I was really in two minds whether to go in. I wanted to. But at the same time I wondered how they'd view me in this place. The snag was my size. Me, I'd have really liked to be mega-tall and everything. Because you can get in everywhere when you're tall. People find it difficult to put an exact age to you. That's something I'd have liked. To be big and strong. It makes life easier in my view. Me, my age, I had the unpleasant feeling of having it thrown back in my face at least thirty times a day. Especially the way some people speak to you. They put on a particular tone of voice, as if you're still sucking your thumb. It's the sort of thing that does me in, that. When I'm old, me, I'll speak normally to guys of fourteen and fifteen. As if they were adults. All of which is a just a way of saying that I went in.

7

I WAS SURPRISED to see it was almost empty. Depression, yet again. I really didn't have any luck. The answer is that I should have gone to a nightclub. People who go out, that's where they must go. It wasn't to taverns, anyway. I went straight to the bar and sat down. Next to me was a guy with yellow hair. Not blond, no. Yellow. It was grey hair that had faded. The sort of guy who washes his hair with an old pair of briefs, if you see what I mean. And his eyes were really translucent. I swear to you. I'm sure that if I were a girl I'd have told you he had really beautiful eyes. A bit like a wolf's. There was an empty glass in front of him. And he was counting what coins he had left so he could buy another. An alky, I said to myself. But the thing about his hair was that it made his face pretty extraordinary. If he'd wanted he could have been an actor. I lit a cigarette, not taking my eyes off of him. His face, it was really quite extraordinary. It fascinated me.

Eventually he noticed me. That's one of my magic powers. When I want someone to turn and look at me I start by staring at them, really intensely sort of thing, and then I keep on. I concentrate, I concentrate, I send out invisible waves, and inevitably the point comes where they turn round, as if they've felt my invisible waves tickling them. I swear to you. It's one of the magic powers I got from an old gypsy. I'm just kidding. Anyway, in the end he noticed me. He picked up his glass, as if to clink it with mine, and made a little gesture. A way of saying hello, like.

A guy like him, I'd have really liked to know his life story. With that hair of his. And especially why his eyes were like that. You got the impression they might start blubbing, these eyes, even for no reason, just for the poetry of it, they were so translucent.

I held out my cigarettes to offer him one. But he said no. So then I gestured at the barman who hadn't noticed me yet, and who made rather an odd face when he saw me, and I asked him, the yellow-haired guy, what he wanted to drink, it was on me. He couldn't get over it that a young guy like me was offering to buy him a drink. He and the barman looked at each other as if to ask if I was joking or what, then eventually he replied: "Ouf, another one then … " The barman turned to me. And I said: "The same." Without knowing what it was I'd ordered. But I didn't care. My drink, I wasn't planning on touching it. I'd already had too much. Even if walking had sobered me up quite a bit.

After that we didn't know what to say to each other, me and the yellow-haired guy. It wasn't easy to get a conversation going. The barman brought our drinks. I was really surprised he didn't ask my age or anything. He must have thought I was over sixteen. That pleased me for a change. This barman, you could tell straight away he'd got class. The yellow-haired guy started knocking it back. I watched him at it. He knew what he was doing. When he put down his glass he saw I was staring at him, it must have made him feel awkward because we still hadn't said anything to each other, and me, my drink, I hadn't touched it, so he said to me: "Looks like things aren't so good … " I pulled a miserable face. To kid him on. If he'd said it looked like things were fine with me, I'd have put on a smile. "No, they're not," I replied. And suddenly I wanted to die. "Oh, life … " he just replied, like you do when you

don't much feel like talking. Then after a silence, he went on: "What happened to you?" I said: "Nothing but hassle." But I sensed that that didn't interest him a whole lot. So when the barman came back I made a sign to him to pay. And I took out my wad of notes right in front of them. That shook them. Then they looked at one another, as if trying to work out where I'd got all this money. And I put my stash back in my pocket, pretending not to have noticed that I'd really impressed them. I swear to you. Once the barman moved away, the guy with yellow hair carried on with our chat. Now I intrigued him. Money, it's terrible how much it can change a person's mind.

"So what are they, these problems of yours?" So then I started telling him all about it. It's true that until then I hadn't been able to talk to anyone about what had happened to me. And when something important happens to you, you feel like confiding in someone. That's natural. Even to someone you don't know. So me, that's what I did. I started by telling him I'd run away from home. But so he'd understand properly, I made it clear right away that I hadn't done it because of my father, seeing he was dead. It was because of the guy who was trying to take his place. And because of my mother, obviously.

That put a damper on things, the fact that from the word go I said my father was dead. But what upset me was that while I was telling him this, I got the impression I was saying something really unoriginal, whereas up till then I'd always had the opposite impression, that what was happening to me was extraordinary, rather like his face.

"What did he die of, your father?"

I don't know what got into me then. Instead of telling him the truth I began altering things. Just a little bit, but even so. It was so he wouldn't be bored, I suppose.

"Officially, he was ill. Lungs. But the truth is it was my mother who killed him."

He opened his translucent eyes wide, like in the horror films. Then he took a long swig from his glass. You've got to put yourself in his shoes. You're having a quiet drink at the bar, and then in comes a guy who offers to buy you another. Okay. And then he gets talking to you, and within three sentences he tells you his mother did away with his father. It gives you the creeps … Then he put down his glass and looked at me with his translucent eyes. I was almost afraid he could read my mind. Some people can do that. I swear to you. Anyway. He looked me in the eye, and he finally asked the question I was waiting for. Namely: how had she done it, my mother. I told him that the bloke she'd moved in with afterwards, he was a doctor, and that it was him who'd claimed he'd died from his lung condition, when in fact it was obvious that my mother had poisoned him. I'd found the tablets she'd used and everything. A kind of rat poison. Just so he'd understand properly, I told him it was me who'd found him dead in the living room, my father, one day when I got back from school. His tongue was sticking out. Like a dog that's been strangled. And that's when I also thought to say that as well as the drugs, he'd been strangled. And that, on the other hand, it couldn't have been my mother because she wasn't strong enough. And so there was an accomplice. And to my mind, the accomplice, it was the doctor she'd moved in with afterwards, and who she expected me to live with. When I said that, it was obviously François I was thinking of.

He looked as if he was completely hallucinating, this bloke of mine. Of all the things he'd heard in his life, it was perhaps the most off the wall. I could see he was thinking

very hard. For example about why he'd been strangled after being poisoned. Generally when you poison a guy, it's not to then have to strangle him afterwards. Unless the tablets don't work quickly enough and you're afraid the guy will have time to tell the police or something. That's what he must have been thinking, my yellow-haired bloke. Any rate, he seemed shocked by my story. And also by the fact that his glass was empty. So I gestured to the barman who immediately got him another. Seeing it was my round. Me, my glass, I still hadn't touched it. "I'm trying to give up," I said to the man behind the bar. Then I carried on yakking to him about my life. It did me a hell of a lot of good to be able to confide in someone. "So what did I do next?" He shrugged. He didn't know what I did next. Me neither, by the way. "I couldn't live with them, knowing what I knew. And my mother, you can imagine how I hated her." His expression said yes. Or he scratched his nose, I couldn't tell. "Frankly, she was the worst of mothers ... The very idea of sharing an apartment with her made me suffer. Really suffer. I absolutely detested her. It was very strained between her and me. Because she knew that I knew. And so we never stopped arguing. She was forever yelling at me. And most of all I had the feeling that my father was watching me through the wall and accusing me of betraying him, if you see what I mean ... I couldn't forget him, my father. He was always there, behind me. Or above, it depended. And I was afraid he'd think I was carrying on living with the woman who'd murdered him without it even troubling me. I was afraid he'd regard me as an accomplice, do you see? It was horrible. So what could I do? That, he still didn't know. But I didn't give him time to answer. Straightway I went on: "I started running away. And I did it so much, run away, that they decided to shove me in a boarding school.

That way at least they'd have some peace and quiet. But it wasn't a boarding school like the others … No. It was called *Black Rocks*. Maybe you've heard of it?"

"It rings a bell," he replied, but I could tell it was just so he wouldn't seem ignorant. Or because he didn't want to contradict me after the life I'd had … "

"It was a terrible place. *Black Rocks*, it's where the world's biggest bastards go when they don't know what to do with them any more."

But since he didn't seem to know too much about it, I described a few episodes I'd been through there, which I got from what my friend Ben had told me, as well as other details I'd heard elsewhere. For example, I told him the problem with the dormitories at *Black Rocks* was that the whole school was in the same building. First years up to seniors. And that the senior years, they often turned up in the first years' rooms for a laugh. Me, when I arrived I was in the first year, and I was subjected to some terrible things for quite a while. Sometimes they smashed your face in. And if you reported them it was worse next time. So no one said anything. But the horror of horrors was the bogs. If you went for a piss at night in the dormitory bogs and you ran into them, they made you do really disgusting things which made you want to die. Me, every Sunday evening before going back to school, I used to shake I was so frightened. It went on like that for two years. Several times I nearly jumped out the window I was so terrified when I heard them come into the dormitory. Especially as the monitor didn't say anything. I never knew why. To cut a long story short, it was really violent. But the most violent of all had to be the leader of the gang, he was called Yann Chevillard. A real bastard. Who made my life hell for over two years, always hitting you, humiliating you in front

of everyone and making you do disgusting things in the dormitory bogs …

He couldn't get over it, this yellow-haired bloke of mine. I hadn't had an easy life. It's true. As I was telling him all this I realised I really hadn't had an easy life. So I was like overcome. After all, it had been tough. But I got through it. Even if it hadn't been easy. He looked at me strangely. I think he was quite impressed. I was almost his hero. Okay. I paused to think up some more ideas, but also to get stuck into my drink. Pouring out my whole life to him gave me a thirst. But it was also a way to stop lying. Because I couldn't have carried on like that indefinitely. I really had to stop for a moment. So I had a drink. But he said: "And then what?" So I went on. It's his fault.

"Then I escaped from this boarding school. I couldn't take it any longer. I was so miserable. But my mother wouldn't listen to a word. She refused to understand that I wasn't happy there. What interested her was having as few problems as possible. And seeing me as little as possible. Basically, she wanted me off her back. Especially as they wanted to have another child, her and her new bloke.

"Oh yeah?"

"Yeah. What's more they had one. The year after. And they gave it the same name as me. As if I didn't exist."

"That's not very nice, that. And what is it, the name?"

"*John*," I replied, out of respect for Jean de La Fontaine.

And we shook hands. But quickly, because I wanted to carry on with the story of my life. It did me a hell of a lot of good confiding in someone. "So, I got myself out of this boarding school. It was a night when I'd been well and truly caught in the bogs by Yann Chevillard's gang.

They stripped me naked. By holding me down by the arms and legs. I was at their mercy. And one of the guys had a knife. I swear to you. Or rather, a Stanley knife. And what they wanted me to think was that they were going to cut my dick off. The worst thing is they'd have been capable of it. They were sickos. He brought the blade closer, and me I was screaming, but there was another of them who put his hand over my mouth so no one could hear me. I really thought he was going to cut it off, the bastard. And then he took his hand away, the one over my mouth so I wouldn't call out, and Yann Chevillard, who was standing over me, started pissing on me, on my face, so I had to shut my mouth, I couldn't call for help. And one of the guys, the one with the Stanley knife, told me to open my mouth if I didn't want him to cut it off. He wanted me to be a urinal, like. And so then I swallowed it all. In short, it was hell."

"So that same night, I'd decided to leave." "How?" I waited a moment to create some suspense. And also to get him involved. But he didn't react. "By going over the wall, quite simply. I walked to the station, it was snowing, and then I got the first train to Paris. I hadn't any money. And I spent the whole journey hiding in the bogs. I was freaking out in case an inspector caught me and reported me to the police. Then, in Paris, I met up again with some people I knew, who were good enough to let me start from scratch and hide me. Because everyone was searching for me everywhere. My photo was on the walls at the railway stations. I was in a terrible situation. If you want to know how I got through it, you just have to read the biography that's been written about me. You'll see that, luckily for me, I met an amazing girl. It's her who gave me my appetite for life back. She hid me in her room. She was much older

than me. Getting into her thirties. Her job, it's teaching French. Anyway, that's what happened … "

He was having hallucinations on the spot. His glass was empty. The barman gave him another without even asking. Then he put one in front of me as well, next to my first, which still wasn't finished. Like my story. So I carried on: "But I had to find something to do with my time, so I began to write. Journalists from all over the world, when I tell them that, they think it's modesty. For them, it can't be boredom that lies behind my talent. They always think there's a better reason. But for me it was simply that. Boredom. And also to unburden myself of the secret that only I knew, ie: that my mother had killed my father … And that he was buried in our garden!"

I was beginning to seriously kid him on. But him, he didn't even realise. Everything I told him he swallowed. To prove it I added: "Under the apple tree!" But he didn't react. And yet he didn't seem stupid.

Just then the barman came back over to us. He put both hands on the bar as if to say that this was his place we were in, and he asked me:

"So you're a student then?"

That annoyed me, him cutting me off in full flow. Especially to ask questions as pathetic as that.

"Not really," I replied. "I'm a writer."

And I looked down, out of literary modesty.

"A writer? What? But how old are you?"

He frowned, as if it wasn't possible for me to be a writer, but at the same time flattered that I should come into his tavern, despite being famous and having an international career. Luckily a guy at the other end of the bar called him, and he went over to him. I turned to the yellow-haired guy. He was struggling to finish his drink. No doubt

he was waiting for the end of my story. Right. But I didn't want to appear the type who does nothing but complain and everything. Because after all, I had quite a lot of luck later on. My books were published. They sold very well. Even better than very well. After all, it's fairly rare to be successful so young. I travelled to quite a few countries for my translations. Pretty much everywhere I'm considered one of the best writers of my generation …

"So everything's fine," he concluded.

It's true I was getting rather muddled up with my success stories. Because after all, I'd begun by telling him that things weren't going very well for me. Okay. But I stuck to it, my success story. But now I had to find something about my downfall. Something that knocked you dead.

"Everything *was* fine," I corrected him. "Everything was fine until the moment I chucked it all away … "

I took a swig from my glass, it was beer, while at the same time asking myself how I'd managed to chuck everything away already. But he wasn't asking me for too many details. He was almost asleep. "Because my obsession," I went on, "was to find that bastard Yann Chevillard. The leader of the seniors' gang. After all these years. And the thing was, Yann Chevillard, he was in Paris. He was twenty. It wasn't hard to find his address. Directory enquiries, that's what it's for! So I found his address. He lived near the Gare Montparnasse. In the rue de la Gaîté, to be precise. When I knew that that was where he lived, I straightway told myself that I was about to make a big mistake. I started roaming around his neighbourhood. And one night I ran into him. I recognized him immediately. Yann Chevillard. I followed him. And when he went into his building, I followed him through the door without him recognizing me or anything. Which shows he wasn't very cultured. Okay, but anyway. He went up the

stairs. And again I followed him. I was a bit stressed. Because I knew I was about to do something really pretty stupid. See, my hands are still shaking too. Oh yes, I forgot to tell you that this was just now … Just before coming here."

I held out my hands, making them shake so he'd see that the episode had really left its mark on me.

"So, I was behind him. On the staircase. Following him. I let him get one floor ahead of me. During the day I'd taken a knife that I found in Madame Thomas's kitchen. The girl I live with. I could feel it in my pocket, the knife. I could feel its appalling weight. To give myself courage I thought about all the horrors he'd subjected me to. And which he'd no doubt subjected other guys my age to. My idea was to make him pay. To make him pay for everything he'd done. A knife in the back. That's what it would cost him. I waited till he got to his door. He put the key in the look. And I was right behind him. Only a few feet away. I could stab him any moment. He was at my mercy. He was astonished at me being there. He turned round … "

Suddenly the barman came back over and interrupted me, just when I was well away, with Yann Chevillard on his landing, and my knife in my hand.

"So, no kidding, it's true you're a writer?"

I made a face.

"Leave him be," said my yellow-haired friend, who seemed to be waking from a long sleep. "You can see he's unhappy in love!"

Unhappy in love.

That knocked me dead.

"Oh? Sorry."

"No no," I said, putting on the expression of a bloke who's unhappy in love. "Anyway, that's life … You have to learn to live with it."

There was an awkward silence. The barman must have thought it couldn't be anything minor, the unhappiness of my love life. Not with the face I was pulling. And it's true that, all of a sudden, I began to feel it inside me, this unhappiness. Suddenly life seemed to be a silly undertaking, a pointless prison, an empty promise. I wanted to die.

"You know what the difference is between playing tennis and making love?" he asked me, probably to cheer me up.

"What?"

I didn't see the connection.

"You know what the difference is between playing tennis and making love?"

"No."

"Well, carry on playing tennis then!" he replied, almost choking with laughter. And joined by the yellow-haired guy.

I couldn't get over it. There was something coarse about their laughter which I found out of place compared with my unhappy love life. Out of place and embarrassing. How could he split his sides when I was on the edge of the abyss? Anyway, no one takes me seriously around these parts. I thought it better to leave a place where people poke fun at your unhappy love life. I paid up and pushed off, offended and suicidal.

I was a bit disgusted. I'd have really liked some extraordinary things to happen. But nothing happened. It was almost dawn. Still, you felt like it was the beginning of a new day. Not quite yet. But you felt it would be soon. I carried on walking along by the Seine. I sat down there, down on the embankment. It was a good hiding place. I'd never felt so much like sleeping. I was exhausted. So I part

stretched out on a bench. Near a weeping willow. I think I slept for a while. But I kept waking up as well. Basically, I was always somewhere in-between. There's nothing nicer, I think. Sometimes I could hear the gulls crying. Because, I don't know if you're aware, but there are lots of gulls on the banks of the Seine which come from Le Havre and which have followed the barges all the way to Paris. Then, when I was properly awake, I went to find a café to have a coffee. Because I didn't really want to be seen. It was daylight. I might be spotted. Especially given my age. Luckily there isn't a soul on the embankments on Saturday mornings. Okay. But I didn't have to look far for a café. I went into a place called Le Frégate, on the other side of the street, and I ordered some breakfast to set myself up again. It did me a power of good. But then I wanted to sleep even more. There were already a few people about, although it was still ultra-early. Because on Saturday, people don't go to work. For the most part they get up much later. As I was thinking that, I realised that that was it then, it was Saturday. My first night without sleep, or almost. Okay. But the thing was I'd got a mega headache. I couldn't think straight it hurt so much. Owing to what I'd drunk. It was almost as ferocious as the first time I got hammered. Having said that, I can't remember the first time I got hammered: I was so pissed.

After that I asked the waiter if there was a small hotel in the area. Since I'd only just arrived in Paris. He directed me to a place a couple of minutes away. L'Hôtel du quai Voltaire, it was called. Off I went, with my headache getting worse and worse. I'd also asked the waiter if by any chance he'd got an aspirin he could let me have. But he said they weren't allowed to give them to customers. I didn't really understand why. But okay. The Hôtel du quai Voltaire, it didn't look top notch as they say, but I didn't care. All I was

interested in, I swear to you, was being able to crash for an hour or two. I went to see the bloke on reception. He looked me up and down. You can imagine the expression I must have had on my face as well. I asked if there was a room available. And I didn't wait for an answer: I straightway got out my card. Well, François's card. I sensed he was uneasy, the bloke. He checked in the register or something. I could just see what was coming. On account of my age and everything. So I felt I had to say something. Like how I'd just that minute arrived in Paris. To meet my publisher-to-be. It was only for the weekend. Then I'd have to go back to Bordeaux. Because of school. He looked at me in a funny way. Then he said: "You've written a book?" I could feel he viewed me differently, the bloke. Impressed to have Julien Parme in front of him. In the flesh. He said I looked young. I shrugged my shoulders, out of humility.

Then he told me my room number, explaining that it looked onto the embankment, but that the windows were double glazed. I said perfect and handed him the card. At that moment I thought that maybe François had already got the bank to cancel it. Stress. I put in the PIN. The guy, he looked at me strangely even so. But I behaved as if I hadn't noticed. So as not to prove him right. Luckily the card went through. He looked reassured. Then he gave me the key.

I went up to the third floor. Inside, it wasn't really very nice. The carpet in the corridor gave you the impression of being in some granny's house out in the sticks. One who's about to snuff it, if you see what I mean. But I didn't care, I wasn't there for the decor. I opened the door to my room, which was tiny. Immediately I went to the bathroom to give my face a quick wash. What I did next was lie straight down on the bed, without even getting undressed or anything. And I fell fast asleep.

PART THREE

THE ELEPHANTS

1

WHEN I WOKE UP I had no idea where I was. It lasted quite a long time. Then I leapt out of bed, and everything came back to me. I hadn't bothered to close the curtains, and the Saturday daylight made me blink. It was almost pleasant. You'd have thought you were on holiday. The first thing I did was have a drink from the tap in the bathroom. At least two litres in one go. Next I lit the last cigarette in the packet, which was also my first of the day. Then I opened the window. Just to smoke in the open air. The sounds from the embankments rose up to me, but out of sync, because of my headache. There was a massive amount of cars now. The traffic was jammed up everywhere. Opposite there was a view of the Louvre and a bridge. It was great, when all's said and done. I stayed there, looking at everything and getting my thoughts straight. What time was it? I rang reception on the phone on the bedside table. They said it was almost two in the afternoon. I couldn't get over it. Two o'clock already! So I'd slept pretty well then. Straightway I thought of my mother. I went back to the window so the whole room wouldn't stink of fags. My mother. By now she must be searching all over for me. The first thing she'd have done was call Marco. To find out where I'd got to. I wanted to call him, Marco, just so he could tell me if there were any developments. I went back to the bedside table and dialled his number, but he didn't answer. Marco, nine times out of ten he didn't answer. It got on your nerves eventually. I thought: 'I hope he doesn't drop me in it with my mother over the business about Madame Thomas'.

Next I took a shower to wake me up completely. It was pretty good really, staying under the shower like that doing nothing. Unfortunately they'd forgotten to give me any soap. Okay. But I'm not one to bear grudges. I stayed under the water for at least twenty minutes. Then I dried myself and wrapped a white towel round me and lay on the bed. I was having trouble getting myself into gear. In the room there was also a little table with writing paper and envelopes. That pleased me. Writers, it always pleases them to see a little table with writing paper and envelopes. On the other hand there wasn't a TV. Too bad. So I thought of writing one to my mother, a letter. To explain. And to say my goodbyes. That was an idea. After that she'd stop looking for me. She'd understand that I wanted to live my life without her. I closed my eyes and told myself that she must be stressing out all over the place, my mother. Because it must scare you, finding your son's not there in the morning. I tried to imagine what I'd do in her place. Obviously, she'd think of asking my friends. And also at Émilie Fermat's. She must have suspected I'd cleared off so I could go to her party. That worried me slightly. I didn't want Mathilde finding out like that. She wouldn't understand. Besides, she'd think I hadn't been straight with her last night. Especially if she got to hear about the business with Madame Thomas. To be honest it was that more than anything which stressed me out. Perhaps it would be better if I told her myself. Besides, that would be an excuse to see her again. Because I certainly had to find one, an excuse. If I wanted to see her again sometime.

I chewed this over for a good little while. I'm never very quick in the mornings. But in any case I didn't have her number. Not her mobile number. Or her landline. Nothing. Marco, he must have her landline. So I tried to get him again, but he didn't answer. Shit. Then suddenly I

remembered she'd told me she went riding every Saturday in Boulogne. Maybe I could go straight there to see her. And talk to her. And kiss her at last. Or write her a letter arranging to meet in the bar of the Hôtel du quai Voltaire. That was a solution too. And above all it impressed me. I went and sat down at the little table. There was a leaflet with suggestions for things to eat that you could have brought to your room. I had a quick look. It was just sandwiches. But in any case I wasn't a bit hungry. I wouldn't have been able to swallow a thing. My throat had a lump in it like a dried-up tap. I picked up some writing paper, headed no less. That way she'd know where to get hold of me. 19, quai Voltaire. It really stood out. A letter that would explain to her that I'd had to leave home, that I was about to go to Italy, but that I absolutely had to see her first. That was good, that was. Then I tried to find the words to say it. But it wasn't easy explaining everything in a few lines. Even for a writer. I got up, dialled Marco's number again, but no joy. So I sat back down in front of my blank sheet of paper. I was even more blocked than usual. But then I launched into it: '*Dear Mathilde* … ' No. That was like writing to a cousin. What was needed was just '*Mathilde*'. I tore up the sheet and got another one, still headed. '*Mathilde* … ' I went to the window to get inspiration by looking at the Louvre. What words came next? And to think that at one time the Louvre was the king's own private pad. In those days they had no worries, kings. They had it easy. Anyway, I'm a royalist me. I remembered that when I was a kid, what I wanted more than anything was to be a prince. I don't know why. There are things that stay around in your head without you knowing why. Most of the time they're pathetic.

I went and sat back at the table. Maximum concentration. '*Mathilde* … ' In fact it wasn't necessarily a good idea to send

her a letter. It's over, the age of letter-writing. Nowadays, we've still got time to write them but we haven't got time to wait for them, so we don't write them any more. '*Mathilde, I'd like you to know* … ' No. That sounded official. The best thing was something mega-brief but precise, so she'd understand that she definitely had to come and meet me here. If not, I'd leave for Italy without seeing her again. My mind wandered to Italy. Venice and everything. Then I got back to business. I tore up the sheet and got another. I copied out the beginning: '*Mathilde* … ' I re-read it several times. For the moment that was it, I'd got the right tone. With letters it's just a question of tone. '*Mathilde, I've got to talk to you*'. Honestly, I've got literary talent. Haven't I? '*Mathilde, I've got to talk to you. For some really complicated reasons, I had to leave home. I won't be coming back*'. Oh my God … I got up, totally fascinated by the power of those three sentences. At the window I repeated three times: "I won't be coming back again. I won't be coming back again. I won't be coming back again … " Then suddenly I added out loud: "ever." And I rushed to the table to immediately write down my 'ever again' before I forgot it. Good ideas, it's always the same: if you don't set them down while they're there, they vanish into oblivion. So: '*For some really complicated reasons, I had to leave home. I won't be coming back ever again*'. Not bad at all. But then I had terrible misgivings. If someone came across this letter, with the letterhead, they'd know where I was hiding. Maybe it wasn't too clever to leave written traces. Besides, to tell you the truth, what I was dreading more than anything was what she'd think of my letter.

It made me think of what had happened with that silly cow Bénédicte, my stepsister, the day I got her to read a short story I'd written. I'll have to tell you about it so you can

understand my problem. It was about three months ago. I'd written a short story. Fifteen pages without crossings-out. Almost a novel, like. I'd read it through about thirty times before coming to the objective conclusion that it was a little gem. The story, it was about a guy who woke up one day having lost his memory. Straight up. And when he discovered what his former life was like, he went mad. Pretty original, to my mind. It was called *A Thousand Years of Solitude*. Which shows you it was really very good. I was mega-proud of it. So what I'd wanted was to know what Bénédicte's opinion of it was. Her opinion, it wasn't really important to me. It's just that I thought she might have something to say to me. Compliments, that kind of thing.

Of course, Bénédicte was never an ultra-cultured girl. She hadn't read La Fontaine, to give you an example. But with this literary short story, *A Thousand Years of Solitude*, I was aiming for the general public. At first I'd even been in two minds whether to call it *A Hundred Thousand Years of Solitude*. That just shows you. Anyway. I'd left it lying around in the living room expecting her to find it. Feigned carelessness, that was my technique. I knew full well she'd read it. That was just her style, reading things that didn't belong to her. Even letters that weren't for her, she'd be capable of opening them.

Sure enough, that same evening my short story had disappeared. I could just imagine her face. Suddenly she realised she'd been living with a genius of French literature for almost two years and she'd never suspected a thing. Under the same roof, what's more. I could already see her coming to cry on my shoulder and asking me to forgive her for having been unbearable to me for the last few months. And I'd tell her: "That's okay, I don't hate you at all."

But no reaction from her. It was getting more and more strange. Then we bumped into each other in the kitchen. I'd been hanging around for at least an hour, keeping an eye out for when she came out of her room. She was pouring herself a glass of milk, calmly, when she said almost absent-mindedly: "By the way, I read your short story." I straightened up, dignified, ready to receive the people's praises. "And?" She finished her mouthful. It put her nose out of joint to be giving me compliments. She put her glass on the table, taking time to find the right words. Because words, she knew now that I was ultra-careful that they should be the right ones. "It's totally useless!" was what she finally came out with. "What?" "It's ridiculous, your story. And anyway, nobody would believe it. Not for a second. No, frankly, it's a load of crap ... "

I knew it ... She hadn't understood a thing. As usual, in fact. It's incredible how this girl remained terminally herself. She never surprised you. She hadn't even understood that the main point of the story, it wasn't the plot, not at all, but the style. Just the style! Except that then she straightway added: "And between you and me, frankly you write like shit." That did me in. I went to wring her neck, but she ran off to her room bleating like a nanny goat. She couldn't understand anyway. Poetry, she'd probably never heard of it. And besides, the text was too demanding for a girl like her. But to be honest, to tell you the truth even, it had got to me a bit. As an artist, I mean. And I wouldn't have wanted Mathilde to think the same thing when she read my letter—which just goes to show that what I write, however hard you try and flush it down the toilet, it won't ever go away.

Suddenly I had the idea of the century. And of the century after that. I picked up the phone again and rang directory enquiries. What I was looking for was the number of the riding club in Boulogne. I preferred to tell her things face-to-face. It was less risky than a letter. Le club du Jardin, it was called. Because it was in the Jardin d'acclimatation. Apparently. The operator asked me if I wanted to be put through. I said yes. Then I got a girl with a rather slurred voice, as if she'd just got up, and I asked her what time Mathilde Fermat had her lesson today. I explained that I was her brother and that she'd forgotten to tell me what time I had to come and fetch her. "At five o'clock," the girl replied. And I hung up, proud of my coup.

After that I left my room. I had shopping to do in anticipation of everything that was going to happen. My first thought was to go back to the rue de Rennes, where I'd seen loads of telephone shops. What I wanted was to buy one. It would be more convenient. I went down the two flights of stairs hoping not to run into the receptionist from that morning. His face didn't really fill me with confidence. So as not to be noticed I went past him without stopping. He just said: "Good afternoon, Mademoiselle." That knocked me dead. But it was because it was actually another man, the receptionist, and I was going so fast that he hadn't had time to see me properly.

Otherwise he'd never have said it.

It did me good to walk in the open air. But at the same time I was really aware of the fact that I was on the run. I swear to you. Every time a car went past I was scared stiff it might be my mother or something, and I immediately turned my head away. As reactions go it was stupid, I admit, seeing there wasn't actually much chance we'd just happen to bump into each other. Paris, it's a labyrinth.

Okay, but there was nothing I could do about it, it was all I could think of. I carried on like that, incognito sort of thing, all the way to the rue de Rennes. And there, guess who I bumped into: not my mother, luckily, but the girl whose name I forgot and who I'd seen the night before at Émilie Fermat's. The ultra-tall blonde who'd been kind enough to let me finish her glass of champers. Everest. She walked past me without stopping. Yet our eyes met. You could bet she hadn't recognized me or anything. But what I told myself was that you're never safe from meeting anyone.

Then I went into a shop. There were quite a lot of people, seeing it was Saturday. The assistants all had the same red jacket. For that reason alone I could never have worked in that sort of shop. Too embarrassing. Okay. But the girl in front of me, she knew nothing about anything. She was asking all the most stupid questions in the world. You might even have thought she was doing it deliberately. It was almost at the level of wanting to know which way up you hold it, a mobile. I swear to you. A real moron. You could bet anything you like it was her first mobile she was buying. She was really moronic. And fat into the bargain. Frankly, there are some people, you wonder how they manage to live. Then another assistant came up to me. I explained to him what I needed. Namely, a pay as you go phone. Seeing I hadn't got any form of identification or anything. In three minutes I'd made my choice. While the other one, the fat girl, she was still there asking why there wasn't a cord on her phone. I swear to you. I went past her to pay, with an ironic little smile. And I wasn't the only one: I sensed the other assistant, the one who was serving her, he wanted to laugh too. But he couldn't, seeing his job was to help her buy a phone after all. Anyway. I handed over

my card. I entered the PIN. But there was a funny noise. "It won't go through," he said. I pretended to be surprised. We tried the process again, but the same thing. So I paid in cash. Fuck. You could bet your bottom dollar, I thought, that François had got his bank to cancel it. It gave me a hell of a scare.

Once I was outside I straightway gave Marco a call. This time he answered. It almost surprised me.

"Marco? It's Julien."

"Fuck, what the hell are you up to?"

He reacted like a shot.

"How's things?"

"You know everyone's looking for you? I don't get it. Where are you? Your mother said you've pissed off. Is that right? Fuck, you could have told me … "

"Don't worry about it … "

"She called me this morning. First thing. She thought you were at my place."

"I'm not that much of a moron."

"But that's just it, you are a real moron. What's got into you? Well? Tell me … Where are you then?"

"I'm not alone," I replied, to get his imagination going.

"You're at Madame Thomas's, is that it?"

"How did you guess?"

"Elementary my dear Watson. But why did you clear off like that? Are you thick or what? We've got to meet up. Come to my place. We'll be able to talk in peace … "

"Too dangerous. We can meet up in a café if you like."
"When?"

"Let's say seven o'clock. I can't make it before then."

"Seven in the evening you mean?"

"Yeah."

"Not before? Right. Okay. Where?"

I thought it best if we didn't meet in a well-known part of town. Just so as not to bump into anyone. The best thing was to get him to come to somewhere not too far from the hotel. I looked round.

"Listen, there's a place called Le Marché. It's in the rue de Rennes. That suit you?"

"Le Marché … that's fine. So, see you in a … "

"Okay. Ciao."

And we rang off. He sounded odd, Marco, on the phone. I imagined he was actually standing next to my parents and everything, maybe with the cops present, and they were all trying to worm information out of him. It sent a shiver down my spine, the thought of it. And I straightway thought that perhaps it would be dangerous to go to this meeting. What I did next was draw out some money with François's bank card. Just to see if it had really been cancelled or if it was just the shop assistant who was a cripple. Actually, in this part of town that was virtually all there was, cash machines. Don't ask me why this one rather than another. And just as I was afraid, it wouldn't let me have any cash. Shit. I ought to have drawn some money out this morning, at daybreak. Before my mother found out I was missing, like. I thought for a moment. On Saturdays Bénédicte didn't usually have school. For me it was a teachers' training day. So no one would have any reason to be up at the crack of dawn. Besides, when I paid for breakfast at Le Frégate it had worked fine. I'd been really stupid not to foresee this. But to my way of thinking, François, he'd have taken longer to find out I'd pinched his bank card. You'd have thought the first thing he did when he woke up was to rush to see if his card had slept alright.

After that I went to a chemist's. I bought some herbal thing to make me feel good. And then a toothbrush. And

a bottle of aspirins. Then I came out of the shop and walked to my hotel. What I wanted was to charge up my mobile. Because from the start it had done nothing but bleep to tell me the battery was flat. On the way I stopped at a bookshop on the boulevard. Sometimes, when I've got time to waste, I like wandering round bookshops. I don't know why, it relaxes me. I had a quick look at what you could buy. And whether by chance there was one of my books. But I didn't stay long. I was dying for a piss. Excuse me for being blunt, but it's true: I absolutely had to get back to the hotel. The thing is that in most novels, they behave as if the characters never went to the bog. As if it was embarrassing. Me, I think that's crazy and totally unconvincing. The novel I'd write, any rate, it won't make out that the characters were all intellect. No. They'll be flesh and blood too. For example, what I find downright annoying is that all the characters in the classics, Racine's and everything, you see them in action for hundreds of years without ever going to the lav. In the end that can't do them much good. They must be doubled up with pain, even. That's why they rant on, on account of holding it back. Centuries of holding it back. There comes a point where it's not possible any more, they have to let something out. Question of pressure. So they rant on. And then people are surprised that they don't know how to play the part and it's not like the way you speak in everyday life. Anyway, I came out of the bookshop and straightway turned left towards the Seine to get back to the hotel.

Once I got there I didn't bother going up to my room. I was only just in time. I went straight to the toilets in the bar, which was on the ground floor. A shiver of relief ran up my spine. Full-on happiness. Then, since I was there, I

asked the guy behind the bar if I could have something to drink. He asked what I wanted, but in a really rude way, so I said apricot juice. Just to get up his nose. Next I sat down in a leather armchair and began flicking through the newspaper that was there. Of course, before that I made sure I plugged my phone charger into a socket that was lying around. Which meant I could switch it on again. It was gone four o'clock by now. When I'd finished my juice it would be time to go, if I didn't want to miss Mathilde at the Jardin d'acclimatation. But to tell her what? That she has an effect on me, for example. That when I see her I'm happy and unhappy all at once. And also a bit ashamed. As if I wasn't good enough for her. Or that she was too good for me. I don't know. And even that sometimes when I see her, I think I need a bath.

But would she even understand what I was talking about?

2

I WENT PAST the guy on reception to get to my room. It was still the same one, with his weasel face and thinning hair. The sort who pays to sleep with girls, if you see what I mean. I smiled at him awkwardly and dashed straight upstairs. The last thing I wanted was to get talking to him. It could have turned out badly. Once I got to my room I dumped my things. I wet my hair and tidied it. I put on some cologne. And I cleaned my teeth. There, that was me ready. I went back downstairs. I could see that the receptionist, on account of seeing me slip past him, was wondering if I was up to no good. As I went out the hotel I wondered which way I had to go to the nearest métro station. A taxi, that was for later. I couldn't afford to keep blowing money all over the place. I had to be careful now. As for direction I got it wrong, and so inevitably I ended up at the Rue du Bac station, which in my view wasn't the closest, but it didn't matter, I'm young, I can still walk.

Then I went on to Concorde, where I had to change for line 1, which would have taken me all the way to Neuilly. In the walkway between platforms I saw a really incredible sight. Something I maybe wouldn't have noticed another time. On a day like any other, I mean. As a result of living normally, I don't know whether you've noticed, but your powers of observation get dulled. You don't feel anything any more. You're quite happy going from one place to another, staring into space. But on days when you feel fragile, your sensibilities are always stronger, your concentration is

as sharp as a knife, and you pick up much subtler things. That's what I think. It's why in my opinion, suffering is a good thing every now and then. It forces you to open your eyes. And conversely, the worst thing to my mind is not knowing how to suffer any more. Some people are like that. You can tell just by looking at them that they're incapable of suffering, of feeling pain, of sinking into anguish. They're always on the surface of things, like a miserable buoy that will never know the depths of the ocean, the fish, the sharks. They're so accustomed to living that they go through the identical days without ever giving a sign of the slightest sensitivity. People like that, they're beyond me. Because in those circumstances I don't see any point in living.

Anyway, the sight I saw was a guy falling over. He was walking along normally. And then all of a sudden, bonk, he fell on the ground. I was behind him. It was strange to see someone fall over. At first I thought he was dead. Sort of heart attack and everything. In fact what was wrong was that he'd just fainted. But it looked serious. Anyway, the moment he fell, everyone gathered round him. An old woman even gave a little scream. And next second about ten people were hovering round the bloke, just to see if he was dead or what. The problem was that mobile phones couldn't pick up a signal. So a young guy said he was going to get help. And away he went at a run. You'd have thought he was in a race, he shot off so fast. Okay. Up till then everything had been pretty much normal. But what happened inside me at that point was I thought about another sight I'd seen in the métro one time, and which had really left its mark on me. I'll explain. So I was in the métro. And at the end of the carriage there was this dead ugly old woman, a kind of tramp who really smelt and who had nothing on her feet. No one wanted to sit next

to her because of the smell. Because when I say she really smelt, I'm not speaking metaphorically: she stank in the true sense of the word, she was so filthy. Anyway, she had one end of the compartment to herself. Me, from where I was sitting, I looked at her and wondered what could be going on in her mind. To be honest she looked slightly mad. When suddenly, same thing, she fainted. She began moaning and foaming at the mouth. I swear to you. Like in a horror film. And yet, and that's what I wanted to tell you, nobody moved. No one. Not even their little finger. And not only because of the smell. Perhaps people thought it was normal, that she often did this, moan and foam at the mouth, and anyway it was no concern of theirs. Except that actually it was their concern, it was staring them in the face with eyes that were begging and saying: help, help me … But everyone shut their eyes. Like it didn't exist. Me, I'd have liked to do something, but I couldn't see what, frankly. I looked round, and as everyone seemed to find it normal I let myself be persuaded. When she could have died, in my view. But I wasn't able to find out, as unfortunately the next station, that was my stop, and I had to get off.

Okay. The comparison I wanted to make was that with the bloke in the walkway, everyone had gathered round right that second. So what I was wondering was: why in one case everyone behaves as if the illness didn't exist, and in the other as if it was the only thing that mattered? The answer is obvious, you can see where I'm coming from, but it's worth enlarging on. It's on account of the shoes. Because the real difference between the bloke in the walkway and the old woman on the métro, is that one had shoes on and everything, while the other was barefoot. In my opinion, to understand someone, almost all you need do is look at their shoes. That's my theory. Reacting to the illness of the bloke

with good shoes who fainted, a member of society if you like, that was just reacting to an illness. Nothing more. It doesn't bother anyone. On the contrary. Whereas reacting to the old woman's, that was something much more. It was to risk being confronted with reality: that there are people who walk the streets with no shoes on. And walking with no shoes, it's the symptom of a much more complex reality, and one which is appalling. I don't know if you see what I mean. Reacting to the mad woman fainting meant forcing yourself to accept the idea that she existed, to remember her, her presence, her state of chaos, her solitude. Things we don't want to see, we don't see them. That too, that's my theory. That's why most people in the métro, I don't know whether you've noticed, but you get the impression they're blind. They can't meet any gaze except their own. Because their eyes face back to front, as if they're trying to look inside themselves. Like ghosts. I swear to you. They could walk past a corpse without even taking any notice. But if you tell them there are people dying at the other end of the world, they're ready to sign all the petitions you want, and to tell everyone it's a scandal.

Me, that's what I call a scandal.

I got off at Sablons. As I came out of the station I saw it was a really lovely day. The sky was bright blue. And the sunlight almost dazzled you. I had to walk another ten minutes before I got to the entrance of the Jardin d'acclimatation. It was ages since I'd set foot in there. In my memory, the last time was actually with my father. But I couldn't remember too well now. Anyway, one time, I remember I'd had a ride on the merry-go-round and that I hadn't been allowed to go on the rest, like the shooting

gallery and everything, although it was that that interested me most of all. The merry-go-round, between you and me, after a while you're just going round in circles. As it is, getting on a horse, me, that really hacks me off, but if on top of that it's a pretend one, you might as well put a bullet in your head. A pretend one, of course.

To get into the Jardin you had to pay. That knocked me dead. Okay, but I wasn't about to quibble over a few pennies. I gave them what they wanted, a gentleman, and used the opportunity to ask where it was, the great Equestrian Club. A girl with gappy teeth like a rodent pointed it out, but I didn't really listen to her, I was so fascinated by her mug which hadn't been near a dentist for ages. It couldn't have been easy for her. Okay, but the person who has it easy, me, I'd really like to meet them. Seriously. After that I didn't dare repeat the question, so as not to upset her, and I hurried off straight ahead, thinking I'd find it eventually, this famous Equestrian Club. I checked on my mobile: it was almost five o'clock. Mathilde would soon be finishing her riding lesson. My idea was to wait for her and suggest she came for a walk in the park with me. After that, if she wanted, I could buy her some candy-floss. And maybe hold her hand. Speed up the pace, like.

In the park, I'd rather tell you straight away: there were quite a lot of people. Mostly families. And lots of children everywhere. They ran past. They whined. They quarrelled. In a way it was like an enormous nursery school. On one side there was also a kind of small river, but really tiny. More like a stream. I walked beside it for at least ten minutes. What's great about this park is the trees. They're all huge. And again I thought that the time I'd come with

my father, they were here even then, those trees, and that for them it was like yesterday, that from their point of view nothing had really changed. So I got the impression we were all tiny. Ants, but with extra worries on our minds.

Suddenly my mobile rang. It made me jump, seeing I still wasn't used to its ringtone. The only person it could be was Marco. He was probably about to change the time we were meeting. Or tell me he'd be late. He was physically incapable of arriving on time, Marco. Even if he tried as hard as he could, Marco, he wouldn't be capable of getting to an appointment on time. It's a sort of illness. Like making up stories. I answered in the voice of someone who already knows what excuse you're going to give him.

"Yeah?"

"Julien. It's me … "

I nearly had a heart attack. I swear to you. It was my mother's voice. I couldn't get over it. I hung up right away. Then I switched off the phone so she couldn't ring straight back. I came close to throwing it on the ground, as if it was burning my fingers. Fuck. How had she got my number? The only possibility was Marco. I didn't see any other way she could have done it. It meant that that son of a bitch had spilt the beans to her. I couldn't get over it. As though he'd set a trap for me. Oh my God, I thought. Friends, you think they're friends, when in fact at the first opportunity they're ready to betray you like nobody. At the time I was devastated. The bastard. In the end there was no one you could rely on. It was his revenge. The thing was, I'd probably humiliated him last night. With my story about Madame Thomas. You could bet your bottom dollar on it. I pictured the scene: my mother, or even the cops, turn up at his place to talk to him, and he pisses himself and spills the lot. The traitor. What made me laugh on the other hand,

but a peculiar sort of laugh, was imagining that maybe he'd also told them the story about Madame Thomas. How I was sleeping with her on the sly. Oh my God …It was getting completely out of control, this business. I imagined the cops turning up at Madame Thomas's to see if I was there. The look on her face, Madame Thomas, when they told her that everyone was in the picture regarding our love story. I'm not kidding, I started laughing out loud all by myself. But it was probably on account of the stress. In any case, meeting Marco, I could forget it. Because meeting him, it wasn't so much a meeting as a trap.

I eventually got to the club, a bit shaken up by all that. I could tell it straight away, the club, from the smell of manure. It's odd, but the only thing I really like about horses is the smell of their manure. To my mind they're the only animal whose shit doesn't stink. You don't hear that said very often. But what surprised me was that I saw some ponies. The kids on them looked scared stiff. As if in fact it was their parents more than anything who wanted them to go riding, thinking they enjoyed it. There was even one girl who was bawling on her mini-horse. She'd got a really small head, with a riding hat on. It made you want to hug her and comfort her. Instead of which her parents were standing at the side busy taking photos of her. I swear to you. Parents, sometimes they're really quite pathetic.

But Mathilde still wasn't there. Perhaps they weren't back from their ride yet. So I sat on a bench just opposite and waited. You should have seen me: I was stressing out like mad over the business with the phone call. To put my mind at rest I told myself it didn't make any difference. No one knew I was here. In this park. Then I got up to buy

something to eat. I wasn't really hungry, although I hadn't eaten all day, but it was just to fill the time. At the side there was a guy in a van who made crêpes and waffles, that sort of thing. Me, what I'd have really loved was an ice cream. Usually I don't like them, but now, I don't know why, I fancied one. I went over. There were four people ahead of me in the queue. It made me depressed, especially over the ice cream, so I went and sat down again. I thought it best to wait for Mathilde and get that sort of thing then. It was nicer. I couldn't see anyone coming back from a horse ride. It was almost ten past five. I was afraid she wouldn't come. Or that I'd made a mistake. But I thought of the call I'd made from the hotel. The girl on the phone had said that a lesson had been booked in her name. So it was fine. Besides, Mathilde had told me the same thing last night. She did it every Saturday, go riding. Suddenly I was afraid it might be Sunday. I had a panic attack, like when you realise on the day of a maths test that you've left your calculator at home. But no, it was definitely Saturday, no problem, all I had to do was wait. So, for a bit of a laugh, I imagined that to earn some money I'd buy myself a van too, like the bloke across from me. What I'd do was be there when school finished, for example. And I'd sell things that people really wanted. Because most of the time, the blokes selling stuff haven't the slightest idea what sort of thing you really want. They sell any old thing. In the métro for example. All those blokes with posters and everything. It's rubbish, frankly. But in any case I couldn't see myself as a salesman. I'd rather be a writer.

Behind me I heard a funny noise in the bushes. I turned round but couldn't see anything. Yet I was quite sure there was a creature or something moving about back there. So I went over to the stream. I didn't know if you were allowed

to walk among the flower beds like that. In my opinion not, but I didn't care. Especially as I'd heard the noise again, which was an animal, I was sure of that now. I went closer. And then all of a sudden there was this mega-furious duck that literally leapt out of the water, quacking for its life. I thought it was mad, the duck. It had scared me to death. But then I realised: on the bank there was a smaller one, a tiny tiny duckling, which didn't know what to do any more. I thought it was really lovely. The mother, she was flapping about unbelievably on the water, going quack quack. I couldn't understand why it had got her in such a panic. And then suddenly she flew off, not very high, just skimming the water, but any rate she cleared off. I thought that was really stupid. Mothers, anyway, they always get emotional over nothing. And so me, I didn't know what to do now.

At first I wanted to go back to the bench. But the feeling I had was that the mother had maybe abandoned him on account of me. I felt guilty. And him, so tiny, cheeping away enough to break your heart. I was afraid I'd made a boob by getting so close. I moved away slightly to see if the mother came back, but no, she'd really done a runner, the bitch. So I went back over to the little one. I picked him up. At first it freaked him out, then he calmed down and I was able to stroke him very gently. It was mad. I could feel his heart beating. And I said to myself: if I squeeze I'll crush him. I wondered what he was going to do now to survive. But then I realised I was probably exaggerating a bit. His mother had just gone to hide. But she was bound to come back. It's the law of nature that a mother takes care of her child. If I left him alone, the duckling, his mother would be back in a few minutes, you could bet on it. So I put the duckling back where I'd found him. Gently and everything. And I slipped away back to my bench.

After that I went straight into the club. Just to make enquiries and not wait around for years for nix. And that's when I saw Mathilde: she was coming out of the stables. Just seeing her, it filled me with emotion. I swear to you. She'd already changed. Or at any rate she wasn't wearing riding trousers. Suddenly, just as our eyes met, she stopped dead, with a tragic look, as if she was trying to work out what the hell I was doing there, then she smiled, which relieved me no end, and she came over to me. My heart was on fire.

"Hi."

"Hi. What are you doing here?"

"Ouf, nothing. I was in the area so I thought I'd come and see you."

"Oh? That's nice."

"Since you said you went riding in Boulogne every Saturday, I thought it'd be an opportunity. I was going for a walk, like."

"That's funny. Have you been to the club before?"

"Not really. I've been past a few times. That's all."

"I'd have liked to show you round, but now I'm a bit late."

"Oh?"

"Yeah. My father's waiting for me."

"He's here?"

"No no."

"And the one you ride, the horse, what's his name?"

"Titan."

Titan. Horses, they always have pathetic names.

"Oh. And so you've got to go?"

"Yeah."

"Would you mind if I came with you to the way out?"

"No. If you like … "

We walked out of the club side by side, but not saying anything. I didn't know where to start. And I was terrified at the thought that, anyway, she was about to go any minute. Her father was waiting for her, that was what she'd said. At reception she gave a little wave to a girl. I told myself that that was probably the one I spoke to on the phone from the hotel. Once we got outside, so we wouldn't have to go right away, I told her about the duckling. I offered to show him to her. She agreed. I'd worked out that she really liked them, animals, Mathilde. I pointed to the bushes. When she saw him she gave a little cry of amazement. That made me happy. "He's really sweet," she kept on saying.

"How old is he, do you think?"

"Don't know. Probably a few days."

I went closer, but she shook her head to tell me not to.

"Don't you want to hold him?"

"No way," she replied.

"Why?"

"You mustn't ever do that. Or else you leave your smell on him. And then his mother won't recognize him. Picking up a duckling takes it away from its mummy forever. And a duckling without a mummy, it's sentenced to death."

"Really?"

"Yeah."

That worried me sick, what she'd just said.

"Are you sure?"

"Absolutely."

Shit. I'd really messed up. But I preferred not to tell Mathilde. She'd have thought I was such a moron. In my mind I told myself I'd see about the duckling later. We came out of the bushes. Then we began walking towards the attractions.

"So it was a good night last night then?" she asked.

"In the end we didn't go to the nightclub with the others."

"Why?"

"Nightclubs, you know, I don't much like them, me."

"Me neither."

"We went for a drink. Then we went home. But mega-late … "

"I was pretty down this morning, me. Especially as I had to help my sister clear up. Some guy threw up in the spare room."

"Serious?"

"Yeah."

"That's disgusting. Do you know who it was?"

"No."

We walked past the rides. What I'd have liked was to suggest we have a go on one. Just like that. For a laugh. And especially to delay the moment when she'd say goodbye to me. But I was afraid she'd think I was immature. So I didn't say anything. Then we started talking about our German teacher. It wasn't a good start at all. She also told me an awful story about her penfriend who lived in Berlin or some place. Basically, her and me, we were talking out of fear of silence, but we didn't say anything really important. Me, what I'd have liked was for us to say important things, but I didn't know how to go about it. Especially with a girl. Girls, anyway, they're pretty incomprehensible. It's been proved by science apparently.

Sometimes I got a bit closer to her. Just a little bit. Our bodies touched, and it was like an electric shock. I thought: Oh my God … Although in fact we were barely brushing each other, and even then it wasn't ever intentional. Then we got to the big dragon. As I didn't know what more to say, I asked her if she'd ever had a go on it. She said no.

So I told her she definitely ought to at least try it the once before she died. That made her laugh, as if I'd got fired up all of a sudden, and she agreed. I couldn't get over it. But she didn't have any money.

"Don't worry," I said. "I'll get this."

And I ran all the way to the place where you bought the tickets. I bought a whole book of them, actually. It was really expensive, but I didn't care: if I had to I'd have given all my money to be with her for a while. Then I ran back to the dragon. For those who haven't a clue about anything, I'll just explain that the dragon is a sort of roller-coaster, except it's a Chinese version. She had a big smile, Mathilde. I swear to you. I think it made her laugh to see me rushing all over the place for something that was really meant more for children. But anyway, she seemed excited. Me too, by the way. The two of us got into the carriage. Two children climbed in behind us. They must have been about ten. In my opinion they were brothers. Because they looked quite similar. The smallest one couldn't get his safety strap on, so I helped him. Then a horn sounded. And the creature began to move.

"Apparently there were some deaths on this ride last year," I said to Mathilde as we set off.

"No?"

"I swear to you. Some people who fell out when it turned over … "

"You're kidding?"

"Yeah."

She began to laugh, then straight away her laugh turned into a shout because we suddenly picked up speed on a really lethal downward slope. The two little boys behind began shouting too. It was even more than shouting, they were screaming. So I started too. As loud as I could. It had its effect, the four of us yelling hysterically. We were going so

fast you didn't have time to see anything. Our hair went all over the place. Especially Mathilde's, as it was much longer than mine. It really blew your mind, the speed. The worst was the final bend: it tilted so far over to one side that it turned your stomach upside down, or at any rate what you had in it. But it wasn't over yet. Because we went back to the start and set straight off again for another go. After a while, when you were used to the speed and everything, it was almost enjoyable. It was like opening a car window on the motorway and putting your head out. All the pressure on your face, it nearly drove you mad. It was freedom, even though you were tied down everywhere. But after a while, I swear to you, you got the sensation that you were flying. Which is what I said to Mathilde, actually. "We're flying, we're flying!" And our screams overflowed into laughter, and vice versa. Then we came up to the death-bend, the last one. Flat out. It scared the hell out of you. And as she screamed louder and louder, Mathilde took my hand. Like someone who's frightened and who's looking for something to reassure them. Except that now, I sensed that fear was just an excuse for holding my hand. And what she did, she did it not as a reflex, but as something she'd been thinking about for several minutes. I couldn't get over it. Even me, I'd have never dared do that. Girls, sometimes they knock you dead.

In the death-bend I screamed with happiness.

Then the carriages slowed down and came to a stop. She immediately took her hand away. We got out of the dragon. Behaving as if nothing had happened. But I could still feel the pressure of her fingers, there in the palm of my hand. And although I'd already done things with girls, even sexual things, at the time, I can tell you, I had the feeling it was the most exciting thing that had happened to me in my life. I swear to you.

3

As we didn't really know what to do next, I suggested we go and buy something. Mathilde, she suddenly didn't seem to be in a hurry any more. We went over to one of the vans. She got a crêpe. Me too. Then we sat on a bench. We stayed like that for quite a while, and it was almost the definition of happiness, although it was much more fragile than a definition, you wouldn't have been able to write it all down in a dictionary, like something conclusive which everyone agrees on. Quite the opposite, it was as fragile as a soap bubble, the slightest little word could make it burst.

"I've got to go," said Mathilde.

"You're meeting your father, right?"

"Yes. We have to do some shopping. I promised him. What time is it?"

"If you like, I'm taking a taxi, me. I'll drop you off. That'll save you time."

She looked surprised. We weren't the age for taxis.

"That'll be great," she eventually replied.

What I'd have loved was to go to the cinema with her. But I didn't know how to suggest it. Still, she'd held my hand. Hey, after all that's a sign, isn't it, when a girl holds your hand? Besides, I was afraid she'd agree, but for a week's time. Next Saturday, to me that seemed like the last day on the calendar. A pigeon came up to us. Mathilde tore off a bit of her crêpe and tossed it to him. The next second there were four or five. Pigeons, I can't stand them, me. If it was up to me I'd exterminate the lot of them, I think. By

throwing stones at their mugs. Fuck. I couldn't wait. In a week's time maybe I'd be at *Black Rocks*. Or in Italy. But you could bet I wouldn't be in Paris any more, hiding.

"Have you been to Italy?" I asked her.

"I went to Rome once."

"Do you think it's nice?"

"Not bad. Why?"

"Because I'm maybe going to have to go there."

"To Italy?"

"Yeah."

"That's great. Why?"

I don't know the reason, probably because of the particular circumstances and everything, and also the fact that she'd held my hand on the dragon ride, but I started telling her about what had happened to me. Steering clear of the details, obviously. I've read Balzac. But I gave her a potted version of the thing about my mother getting married. Of Bénédicte, who hated me. Of the fact that I was basically on my own. Left to my own devices. A runaway. I told it all. She listened to it all in silence. I wondered what she'd think about it, frankly, all this business. When I finished she just asked:

"And you're not planning on going back?"

"I can't now."

"You think?"

"Yeah. It's impossible. It's too late."

"But you'll get caught some time or other."

"I know. That's why I'd like to see Italy first."

As I told her that, I was filled with emotion. I could feel my lower lip start to tremble. But I controlled myself, sharpish. I don't think she saw anything. At any rate, she didn't say anything for quite a while. Then she got up. I thought I was going to die. And we started walking towards the way out.

I did the same as her, obviously. I was afraid I'd made a boob by giving her the truth. But as we walked she told me a story. About how at one time her sister Émilie used to run away quite a lot. Especially during the holidays. And one year, four years ago, something particular had happened. From what she said their parents weren't divorced at the time. And they'd all gone to the Île de Rê together. As a family, like. They stayed in a hotel. The two sisters in one room, their parents in another. Back then their father was much stricter than he was now. Émilie and him, they didn't get on at all. Particularly as he wouldn't let her go out at night, even though her friends, they were allowed to. So she often met up with them secretly, after midnight. But her, Mathilde, she didn't know anything about it, seeing Émilie waited till she was asleep before she went out. She did a bunk, basically. It was in July. At night, the place where everyone went dancing was called La Pergola. A nightclub, but outdoors. Right. And so one time, Mathilde had woken up in the middle of the night and found her sister wasn't there. She'd started freaking out. The first thing she thought was that maybe something had happened to her. She waited for a while. To see if she'd come back. Then, because she didn't know what to do next, and also because she was ten, she went and knocked on her parents' door. And that was when the drama had begun. Their father had got dressed. He'd taken the car. And he'd gone round all the nightclubs. He was hopping mad, their father. And after a while he obviously went into La Pergola. That was where he thought he'd find her. And he wasn't wrong.

Émilie was dancing when she saw him some way off, looking for her everywhere. It must have given her a shock. To see her father when she thought he was fast asleep at the hotel. The fright of her life, probably. She just had time

to get away before he saw her. She hid in the bogs. But her father recognized some of his daughter's friends, and he wanted to know where she was. They all said they didn't know. Real friends, like. The opposite of Marco. Him, in their place he'd have said: "She's in the bogs, she's hiding, it's at the end there on the right, and if you want her new mobile number, this is it." They'd lied and her father had believed them. Émilie wasn't in this nightclub. That's why he went back in the end, her father, in a panic about all the things that might have happened to his eldest daughter. He waited all night in the hotel room. Mathilde, she'd never seen him like that, he was stressing out so much. Right. For her part, Émilie, she didn't dare come back now. Seeing she knew she'd get a roasting. 'I'm going to be murdered', she must have thought. And she wasn't wrong.

In this story, anyway, no one was wrong.

One of her girlfriends offered to let her sleep at her place, she accepted for the first night. But the next morning it was still the same story, she daren't go back. And the more time went by, the less she dared. Her father went to the cops. They started an investigation. Especially as the year before there'd been some business with a girl who got raped on the Île de Ré. Things began to take on nightmare proportions. And her girlfriend told her she had to leave. Émilie spent the next night on the beach. Right. And finally, next morning, she went back to the hotel in tears. Her hair filthy and everything. And ashamed. But the moment her father saw her, instead of giving her a clout or yelling at her as you might have expected, he ran up and hugged and kissed her. He called her 'my darling'. He even cried, holding her really tight and telling her: "Never do that to me again … " According to Mathilde, that was when they started to get on well, Émilie and her father. And to love each other, even.

I wondered why she was telling me this story. Maybe to let me know I was making a mistake when I said I couldn't go home again. To tell me, contrary to what I thought, that no one would murder me on the spot. It's possible. Except when you know my mother, who's really hard and strict and everything. Because you'd still have trouble imagining her as someone who hugs you and says nice things to you, my mother.

"And what are you going to do?" she asked again.

"Don't know."

"But where are you sleeping?"

"In a hotel."

I got a blank sheet of paper from my pocket. As if I needed proof. She looked at it: it was the headed paper from the Hôtel du quai Voltaire. She thought for a moment again.

"But have you got enough money?"

I was in two minds whether to tell her I'd nicked François's card, his bank card, but at the last minute I stopped myself: it was perhaps something to keep to myself.

"I'll manage."

Anyway, we were talking about important things at last, and it was really good. The problem was that we were already at the way out of the Jardin. In life, the things you think are nice, they never last long enough. I felt sick at the thought of soon saying goodbye to her without knowing if I was going to see her again sometime or what. A free taxi was waiting just by the exit. But we'd only just got in when she gave a little cry, sort of like a sleepy dormouse.

"What's the matter?" I asked.

"I forgot my bag."

"Where?"

"In the club. Damn! I left it in the box. I'll have to go back."

"Couldn't you get it next time?"

"No. It's important. I'm so stupid. It's got my purse in … "

"Wait here in the taxi. I'll run back. It'll only take me a minute."

"You sure?"

"No problem."

The truth is I was happy to do her a favour. Besides, I really liked that, the idea of a girl waiting for me at the edge of the Bois de Boulogne. Anyway. I got out the taxi. I explained to the girl at the entrance, the rodent, that I'd left my things inside. She let me in. Then I started running like mad. I imagined what might be in her bag. A pair of panties, maybe. I couldn't get over it, everything that was happening to me, these extraordinary adventures. I got to the club. She'd told me that the loose box, it was Titan's.

Titan.

I asked a girl where they were, the boxes. She pointed them out vaguely. The next minute I was searching among the horses' names. Titan. I opened the stable door. Luckily it was empty. In the hay at the side I straightway spotted Mathilde's bag. I picked it up, child's play, when suddenly I felt a hand on my shoulder. It really made me jump. I turned round.

It was Bénédicte.

I nearly had a heart attack. She scared me so much. She was in her riding outfit, the bitch. And in a fraction of a second I realised she belonged to this club too. Fuck.

"What the hell are you doing here, Julien?"

"Nothing."

I must have gone all pale. I felt the colour of fear spreading across my face.

"Where have you been? Everyone's worried! Are you stupid or what? Why did you go off like that? Your mother's going insane … where did you sleep?"

She came towards me. And so me, I backed away towards the wall. I was caught, like in a trap.

"Keep away from me."

"You have to come home now."

She had a murderous look in her eye.

"Keep away, I said."

"What are you doing here? At the club?"

I almost said: "I came to see you." But I wasn't in the mood for jokes.

"Leave me alone. Let me go!"

I tried to push her away but she wouldn't let me.

"No. You're staying here. I'm going to ring our parents."

"Do that and I'll kill you."

"You don't understand, do you?"

"It's you who doesn't understand."

"You little bastard you."

"Clear off."

I shoved her. But she grabbed hold of me like a lunatic. I swear to you. She wouldn't let go of my sleeve. And she started hitting me with the riding crop in her other hand. As if I was a horse. It really hurt. I backed away. I had the feeling the trap was closing on me. Fuck. And to think that Mathilde was waiting for me in a taxi two minutes away. I tried to calm down, despite the rage she'd stirred up in me.

"Is that it then, are you happy? You've hit me with your crop. Do you feel better?"

"You're a real loony, my lad."

"Too right … "

"Anyhow, I've always told you you'll end up like your father. In the loony bin."

The familiar tune from Bénédicte was to hint that my father hadn't died of cancer like my mother had told me, but that he was in an asylum sort of thing. I knew full well it was totally untrue, but at the time it made me wild. So I shoved her again so I could get past. She screamed. Like hell. Then she gave me another whack with her crop, partly on the face. I could feel she'd cut me somewhere. Anyway, it hurt like mad. Especially as I could see she was about to do it again. She'd have hit me like that until I calmed down and they put the cuffs on me. So, to make her let go and stop attracting everyone's attention by screaming, I punched her on the nose, but like mega-hard. It had the desired effect. She fell on the ground. And she stayed there, not moving, sobbing and holding her nose which was pissing blood. I straightway picked up her crop. I made as if I was about to hit her, honestly I was within a fraction of it, and said: "Say that again, what you just said. Say it … !" I could hear my breathing, it was like an animal's, a racehorse, tensed-up and everything, my nostrils were all dilated, and I concentrated on not hitting her, because I sensed I was on the verge of punching her hard again, but in the end I lowered my arm and just added: "You leave me alone now, right? Let me get on with my life in peace." She was still bawling. She turned to me. She couldn't even make a proper sentence, everything was so mixed up: her blood, her breathing, gasping, sobbing, her insults. She was a pitiful sight. Then she started over again: "You'll end up in an asylum, I tell you. With your father. Because that's where he is, your psycho of a father … " I couldn't bear it. I gave her another punch in the face. There was a crunch. I was afraid I'd hit her too hard. That I'd rearranged her

face for her. I wasn't sure whether to call someone or not. Or to help her get up. But in the end I took off. Out of fright. Behind me I could just hear screams. Louder and louder. Appalling screams. Like a woman in labour. And who's being raped by pain.

After that I started to run, run, run. I didn't know it was possible to run so fast. And the more I ran the more I realised what I'd just done. Fuck. I'd gone too far. The taxi was there. I got in and straightway told the driver to take us to the Champs. Mathilde looked at me strangely. The expression on my face must have been alarming or something.

"What is it?"

"Nothing. Nothing."

I turned and looked out the back window to see if anyone had followed me or what. Nobody. My heart was beating like crazy. As if I'd killed someone. I swear to you. It was the same sensation. Unfortunately our taxi was blocked in. The car in front was in the way.

"Quickly," I said.

I turned round again. This time I saw two blokes running in our direction.

"Shit."

"What's the matter, Julien?"

"What the hell's it up to, that car?"

"Well I can't drive over the top of it!" said the moron of a driver.

"Nothing's the matter," I told Mathilde, faking a reassuring smile, and I gave her her bag.

But I saw her looking at my knuckles. Then at my cheek, which was stinging slightly. She saw the blood.

"You've hurt yourself? What happened?"

"I'll tell you in a minute."

The car in front began to move slowly. Actually it was trying to park. But the girl at the wheel was making a wank job of it.

"Blow your horn!"

"What difference will that make?"

Behind us the two blokes were already coming out of the park. One of them looked in my direction. It really scared me. So I lay down. I put my head on Mathilde's lap. She turned round. She saw the two guys. And she understood, I think.

"You can get past now," she told the driver.

"Just a second, just a second … "

The car in front simply couldn't back into the parking spot. So it gave up. Which left us room to get out at last. Just as we started moving I sat up. I saw the two guys looking everywhere, to the right, to the left, but they got smaller and smaller until they didn't exist any more. I swear to you, I'm not making it up. That's what happened.

4

I DIDN'T KNOW what to do next. As we drove I calmed down
a bit. You have to understand that the whole thing, it had
happened very fast. Because now I'm taking my time to tell
you and everything, but the way it happened for real was
mega-quick. No time to get your breath back or anything.
Gradually my emotions settled. Like the dust. The driver
turned on the radio. I put on a phoney smile for Mathilde.
She gave me a questioning look. I wasn't really sure whether
I should tell her the truth. I thought it best not to. Even if I
realised that she'd find out anyway. Seeing the whole club
was bound to hear about it, what had just happened. Within
a week at most she'd know everything, and she'd think I was
a thug. I was a bit ashamed. But at the same time, she'd got
in my way, Bénédicte, and she'd hit me in the face with her
crop. She was a public menace, that girl. I put my hand to
my cheek which was still stinging as much as ever. I got the
feeling I was going to have a scar. What I find strangest, now
I think back on all of it, is that I never guessed Bénédicte
might be a member of the same cosy club as Mathilde. To
me, Bénédicte, I imagined her in the other club I'd been to
with her a couple of times right at the start, and that club,
as far as I remember, wasn't in Boulogne. Basically, I hadn't
been careful enough.

I launched into some cock-and-bull story. My first
thought was to tell her that when I got to Titan's box, some
guy had already opened her bag and was about to pinch it.
And as he wouldn't give it back, we'd come to blows. Okay,

but it was no-way convincing, especially as the moment I started telling her all that I got another idea, a better one, a watertight one. I told her that on the way I'd bumped into a guy I'd dreamt of bumping into again for years: ie: Yann Chevillard. I swear to you. So then I had to explain to her that, to cut a long story short, he was someone who'd given me a really hard time when I was a teenager, about ten or eleven. He'd been so sadistic to me back then that I'd sometimes got to the point of wanting to die. No kidding. So I'd recognized his face, and I hadn't been able to resist: I'd called out to him to make sure it really was him, he'd turned round, and so then I'd given him the best punch of my life. For old times' sake, if you like. But since he was a tough one it hadn't been enough. It was Achilles against Hector. Especially since he'd got a riding crop. He came out of the club. And we really laid into each other. A punch-up that deserved to be in an X film, I told her.

She seemed convinced. Me too, I might add. In telling her all that, I almost believed it was the truth. A feeling of intense joy welled up inside me, as if after all these years I'd finally made up for the humiliations he and his mates had put me through. In all this business I came out on top, even if it had taken me a while. I'd got my own back, but without ill-feeling or anything. Just with the idea of putting right what he'd damaged. Getting justice, like. It's true: I felt all that as if it were the truth. But now I think it probably was true as well, except that Bénédicte acted as a substitute, and that somewhere deep down inside me, the punch I'd given her was actually aimed at Yann Chevillard.

We went all the way back up the avenue like that, the one that leads to the place de l'Étoile. I felt like a hero after my

story. It couldn't have been better in a dream. Even if I was still in shock from what I'd just done. In real life. And that secretly I was trembling all over. But my consolation was sensing that Mathilde was quite impressed. I'd really got my self-confidence back. If it came to it I'd have been capable of making her believe that the Unknown Soldier at the Arc de Triomphe was actually my father. I swear to you. At that moment, the difference between the truth and a lie was no longer of any importance. It was a dividing line that didn't mean anything any more. The only thing that mattered was that I was in a taxi with Mathilde, that we were a few inches away from each other, and that a moment ago she'd held my hand.

Once we got to the Champs she took out the blank sheet of paper I'd given her. She read out:

"Hôtel du quai Voltaire. Why there?"

"By chance."

"You've got a TV in your room?"

"No. But I hate TV anyway. They're a load of cretins on TV."

"Whereabouts on the Champs?" put in the driver, who was a total pain in the arse.

"Rue Pierre-Charron," Mathilde replied.

"We're nearly there."

"I know."

I spotted the pizzeria from the night before. It made me feel nostalgic, as if I was remembering something from a really long time ago.

"What would make me awfully sad," I dared tell her, "is if we weren't able to see each other again."

She thought for quite a while.

"Were you serious when you said you wanted to go to Italy?"

"I think so. Yes."

"And when are you going?"

"Tomorrow maybe."

"So soon?"

I took my courage in both hands.

"So do you think we could meet up again a bit later, after you've been shopping?"

She thought for quite a while again. I said we could go to a film, for example. Or somewhere. Then she said she'd try. Seeing it was the only way for us to meet up again. But first she had to sort it out with her father.

"It's best if you don't tell him we've seen each other," I added.

I knew full well that my mother was making her own investigations behind my back. It wasn't her style to sit twiddling her thumbs until I came back. And it could be that she'd already warned Mathilde's father. After all, the last time I'd been seen was at their place. In short, we had to be extremely careful. She said it wasn't a problem: her father, he happily let her go out. Authority wasn't his style.

"We can just meet up at my hotel. That'll be the simplest."

"What time?"

"Don't know. How about nine o'clock."

"Great," she finally agreed, with a wonderful smile.

"What number?"

This driver, I'd have really liked to cut him out of the picture.

"Thirteen."

"Here we are then. This is it."

"Me, I'm going on," I said.

Mathilde looked into my eyes for a long time. A girl you

love who looks at you like that, it can knock you dead on the spot. Then she asked for my number, in case she had a problem. She put it in the phone book of her mobile. I thought that was an ultra-good sign, actually. After which she ran off. Like a doe. I didn't know what to think any more, except that I was madly in love. It had happened to me before obviously, but never quite like this. This whole day, when you think about it, it was turning out to be incredible. I was so nervous at the thought of seeing her again that night, but at the same time really excited. In a hotel, on top of that. I put my hand to my cheek again. It was stinging badly.

I asked the driver to drop me at my hotel. During the drive I imagined what must have happened at the club after I left. It made my stomach churn. To my mind, they must have had plenty of things to treat it with, her pious little mug. Girls who ride horses often hurt themselves. On account of falling off. They must have an amazing first-aid kit. Designed for far worse cases than a whacking great punch on the nose. Maybe I'd bust it, her nose. The bone I mean. Otherwise she wouldn't have bled so much. I hope not, I thought. Talking of first-aid kits, Bénédicte had once told me a story which, in my opinion, had genuinely happened. A girl at her club was picking something up off the ground when a horse trod on her hand, basically. The girl, she'd had her finger chopped off. I don't know if you can imagine it. She screamed blue murder. And they sent her to hospital straight away. But the rather revolting thing was that the person in charge of the club told them all they had to find the piece of finger which must be lying round somewhere in the mud.

Because apparently it could be stitched back on. And so all the girls from the club got down on their hands and knees to look for the piece of finger, and the one who found it, yes, it was Bénédicte.

If I'm telling you all this, it's to say I wasn't too worried about her nose. They'd take care of it on the spot. On the other hand, she must have got them to call our parents. I could already imagine my mother's reaction. I'll remind you that she'd told me I'd turn out for the bad when she'd discovered I smoked. So if she found out I'd hit my fake sister, then she'd be capable of reporting me to the police herself. In any case, after this they'd be after my scalp. Especially François. Seeing the punch I'd given her, his daughter, was a right corker. To tell you the truth, I'd never have believed I could do it as hard as that. But in my mind I hadn't really decided what had happened. That was how it had turned out. Then and there. For example if I'd asked myself the question: "Do you want to punch her?", I'd have very likely said no. Basically, it happened all on its own. It was because of what she'd said about my father. But my first thought, you have to believe me, wasn't to bust her nose at all. Because when you think about it, busting your sister's nose isn't nothing. Said like that it scares the hell out of you. So the truth was I was a violent bloke. It had never occurred to me, but now I suddenly realised I was a violent bloke.

The driver dropped me off opposite the hotel. I was beginning to seriously have guts ache because I hadn't eaten anything all day except for the crêpe just now. Yet I wasn't a bit hungry. Quite the reverse. That's why I didn't want to get anything to eat. On the other hand, what I did

want was a packet of cigarettes. Instead of going to the hotel I walked round the area to find a bar that sold them. I was really stressed out. But it took some time to find it, this bar, seeing the district was overrun with art galleries. In the windows that's all you could see: paintings, paintings and yet more paintings. But no cigarettes. Eventually I found a sort of newsagents. I went in, and since there were a few people at the till I had a squint at the papers and magazines. I thought it would be a good idea to buy some, seeing I'd got quite a while to wait. I had a little look at what they'd got, which I'd sum up as: spoilt for choice. I picked up a copy of *Entrevue*. On the cover there was a quite pretty girl, almost naked, and written underneath: '*What women want.*' Right. Instructive, like. Nearby there was something else I'd have really liked to buy, which was *The Life and Times of Scrooge McDuck*. Now obviously, I'm fourteen. I know that. In itself, sure, I wasn't really the age for it any more. I was well aware of that. I'm not a moron. And it wasn't too impressive, I think, to go to the till with a *Scrooge McDuck*. The girl would take me for retarded. And if there's anything I can't stand, it's being taken for retarded. The girl, if I turned up at the till with a *Scrooge McDuck*, the last thing she'd imagine would be that the guy in front of her was meeting a girl in a hotel that same evening. And that on top of that he was the dangerous sort.

In a newsagents, there are two things that are really difficult to buy for a guy my age, and that's *The Life and Times of Scrooge McDuck* and a porn mag. Discreetly I went over to the adult shelves, although taking care not to be noticed too much. I got the feeling I was standing in front of a gold mine. My theory is that to dare to pick up one of those magazines and take it to the young woman at the till, you've really got to have bottle. Because obviously the

young woman gives you a funny look, and you can tell from her eyes that she thinks you're a filthy disgusting pervert. Although between ourselves I don't see what's disgusting about flicking through one of those magazines occasionally. Okay. But the tricky thing is being able to look at them without getting caught by everyone. My dream would've been to be able to have a good look at those magazines once and for all. Just to make sure they didn't interest me. Because the truth is, and I'd like to make it clear to all my female readers, that that kind of magazine doesn't really interest me. Not at all, even. I swear to you. But to be quite sure you definitely need to check occasionally.

To conclude, I went to the till. I asked for a packet of menthol cigarettes. Straight out. Menthol ciggys, I don't love them. What's more, a few people told me they make you sterile. Okay, but I also heard that for your breath they're still the best thing going. Don't forget I was meeting Mathilde, and that when it came to breath it was better to take precautions. If you see what I mean. After getting the fags, the next thing I did was put my magazines on the counter. Self-confident sort of thing. First *Entrevue*. The one with the naked girl on the front. Then, on top of it, and to make sure it was hidden, *The Life and Times of Scrooge McDuck*. Then, to sweeten the pill, in other words so I wouldn't be taken for a mentally retarded kid, I also asked if they'd got *Le Monde*. Well clearly they'd got it. It was on the side. I quickly grabbed one and put it on top of the pile.

"Will that be all?" the girl asked.

5

I WALKED OUT with all that lot. On the way I switched on my mobile to see what time it was. I knew I had a fair while to wait before she arrived at the hotel. But I preferred to make sure. Immediately the phone rang. Fuck. There are things in life which don't make you happy. It was my voicemail. I listened to the beginning: 'You have four new messages … ' Then I hung up. Frankly, I had no intention of listening to them. My mother must have been making death threats. And Marco perhaps, who was wondering why I didn't show up at Le Marché. Too bad for him, he'd be waiting a long time. But maybe the bastard wouldn't even have bothered to go. Thinking I was about to get caught by the cops or someone. Still, all that little lot could wait for me, they weren't that far away: four or five streets from here, if you think about it. Then, so as not to think about it any more, I decided to switch my phone off again.

At reception it was still the guy I'd seen a bit earlier who'd thought I was a girl. From behind, just to be clear about it. He gave me a mongoloid smile. Then he asked if I'd had a good day. I said: "Incredible." But he straightway gave a funny look, and I realised it was because of the cut on my face. Judging by his expression it couldn't have been a pretty sight. I quickly got my keys and went upstairs without hanging about. Once I was up there I lit a menthol with hotel matches. That's what I really like about hotels, they always leave tons of matches everywhere for you. To saying nothing of the ashtrays. Next I quickly washed my face. I'd got a

nice old cut, and it was stinging more and more. After that
I lay on the bed to give some thought to how I was going to
arrange my evening. Then I picked up the room phone and
asked directory enquiries for the number of SNCF. They
put me through and almost immediately I got an adviser.
What I wanted was the times of the trains for Italy. The
girl asked me which destination. Off the top of my head
I said: "Rome." And she searched on her computer. Then
she asked when I wanted to leave. I said: "Sometime around
midday. Tomorrow." There was one at twenty-past twelve
actually. From the Gare de Lyon. Changing at Lausanne.
And a couchette after that, all the way to Rome. I said perfect,
noting the departure time on the hotel notepad. Twenty-
past twelve, Gare de Lyon. My ticket, she suggested I buy it
direct over the phone. But I thought it best not to. Anyway,
I didn't have a credit card now. And anyway, I'd have never
done that. So that no one could pick up my trail.

What I did next was open the minibar to see what was
inside. But it was a minibar: when it came to champagne
it was on the stingy side. So I went downstairs to ask for a
bottle, as well as two glasses. Champagne glasses, I said to
be precise. To be charged to my room. The guy promised
to bring me up all the trappings. Hotels, I love them. And
I went back to my room, more and more chilled-out. But
at the same time more and more tensed-up at the thought
that I was soon going to see Mathilde again. In barely an
hour-and-a-half. I thought back to the night before, that
I'd spent walking outdoors without knowing where I was
going. Compared with the one coming up, it was sheer
horror. I opened *Entrevue*. Well then, tell me all about it,
what do they prefer you to do with them, girls? I searched
every page for the answer to the question on the cover.
What there was mostly was quite a lot of naked girls, but

only partly naked. Nothing obscene, I mean. But as for an answer, I could always keep looking. Anyhow, I don't see how anyone could tell you what you should do with a girl. Because first of all that depends on the girl. And besides, it also depends on her age. For example, I'm sure there are things that some girls really like that others don't. That's why, in my view, you shouldn't try to understand. Me, anyway, I don't understand a thing about girls. The only thing I do know is that them, they can understand us really well. Although that's not difficult.

Then someone knocked at the door. It stressed me out. I straightway thought of my mother. And I hid the magazine under the pillow. It's pathetic, I admit. Okay. But I went to open it. It was the guy from the bar. He was bringing the bottle. Above all he'd thought to shove it in a bucket for me, with ice and everything. It was definitely quite a sight. And the two champagne glasses I'd asked for. He put it all on the desk. I thanked him a dozen times, promising myself I'd remember him when it came to tips before I left France. Then I went back to my reading, but the truth is it wasn't even really as good as *Scrooge McDuck*. That's why I ran a bath, and when it was full to overflowing I slipped in with my cartoons. The one I like most is the big adventure on the centre pages, with Scrooge, Donald and Huey, Louie and Dewey. And the burglars who never get anywhere. Morons, like. It made me laugh. I don't know why, but reading it in the bath, that made me happy. It's not my fault, I'm nostalgic.

By the time I got out the water was cold and I'd finished the magazine. For once I'd made a special point of using soap. You never know. Then I put the same clothes back

on from during the day. What wasn't encouraging is that
Mathilde had already seen me like that the night before,
and again this afternoon. Basically, she was going to think
I never changed my clothes. But at the same time she knew
my particular situation. That was ancient history. My
Scrooge McDuck, I put it in a cupboard with *Entrevue*, well
hidden, and left *Le Monde* where it could be seen. On the
table. Next I opened the window to let in some fresh air.
And I took advantage of that to have another cigarette and
look at the Louvre. My face was still hurting, which made
me think of that turd Yann Chevillard again. The fight to
the death we'd had on his landing … And straightway I
thought I'd ring directory enquiries. Just to see. He must
have still been living with his parents, the bastard. Which
means I just asked for "Monsieur Chevillard". They gave
me three addresses in Paris. You could bet he lived at one
of them. I made a note of them without really knowing
why. One day, I told myself, I'll find him and I'll bump
him off. I closed my eyes and imagined smashing his face
in. He'd suffer, Yann Chevillard. Because I was a violent
bloke. But more than anything I was thinking it for the sake
of it. I knew I'd never do it. Yann Chevillard, I didn't give a
toss about him now. He was part of another life. The time
when I'd been really persecuted by morons.

Next I switched on my mobile to find out the time. Once
again the voicemail rang. This time I had five messages.
I was afraid the last one had been left by Mathilde. No
kidding. So I decided to listen to it, but by systematically
skipping over the others. When I got to the fifth one I
recognized my mother's voice. I scarcely gave her time to
say my name before I deleted the message by pressing '2'. I
didn't even want to hear the sound of her voice. I was too
afraid of what I was going to hear. She must have known

about the business with Bénédicte. But strangely I was relieved that it was her, this message. My worst nightmare would have been Mathilde cancelling for some reason or other. It was almost eight thirty.

Lying on the bed, I imagined her getting ready. Girls, I don't know if you've noticed, but they're really clothes-conscious. Sometimes far too much. To my mind, she wouldn't turn up wearing the same outfit she had on earlier. That's why I could see her in front of the mirror, trying on different dresses. And maybe even looking to see which of her bras would make her chest look the nicest. Me, I don't know if I've already told you, but girls' breasts, they almost drive me nuts.

I switched on my mobile. Eight thirty-six. I turned it off.

Then I thought about Italy again. The first person who talked to me about it, Italy, was Madame Morozvitch. From what she'd told me she'd lived there for quite a few years. On account of her husband who worked in I don't know what now, but in Italy. Me, what I'd like, would be to go and stay by the sea. Not far from Capri, if you see what I mean. I could easily come up with a scheme for earning some money. And I'd stay there, where the weather's always good. Thinking about all that gave me the idea of going to see Madame Morozvitch. She was in an old people's home somewhere near Versailles. I wondered if you could visit her on a Sunday. Probably yes, seeing that families, it was mostly weekends they could come and see their old folk. Even if I'd heard that most of the time they didn't come and see them much. Old people's homes, that's exactly what they're for. Me, at any rate, it's something that makes me really sad. At the end of the day I find death much more

appealing than the corridors of an old people's home. At any rate, when my time comes I hope I'll have the courage to go before I end up as a vegetable in an undertakers' waiting room that smells of piss.

Eight forty on my mobile.

I got up and sat at the desk. I'd just had an idea. In fact I wouldn't have time to drop in at the old people's home. Seeing my train was at twenty-past twelve and I probably wasn't going to get up at the crack of dawn in the morning. There was no point dropping in for two minutes. Especially since Versailles wasn't next door. The best thing was to write to her. So I sat at the table, I pushed *Le Monde* aside, and I began with the intention of telling her that I was going to Italy, and also to thank her for having taught me to really like books and everything. In fact throughout the whole of this business it was her who'd been the most decent. I hesitated for quite some time over whether to tell her I owed her rather a lot of money. I even thought of sending her some of what I'd got left. At least that way I'd have squared things up with everyone before leaving. But I knew very well I wouldn't do it. It was just for the idea. To give myself the impression of having thought of it. And anyway, it's too risky sending cash through the post. I know someone who got fleeced like that. Postmen, frankly, they don't let anything through. Before delivering a letter they always hold it up to the light to see if there's a note inside. It's well known. Get a note, put it in an envelope. If you send it by post you can be sure that's the last you'll see of it. So I couldn't pay her back. Still, she couldn't have done anything with it in her old people's home. And you could bet your bottom dollar that it was her son who'd collect the lot. That, no thanks. Him, he was a real cunt. He didn't realise how lucky he was to have Madame Morozvitch for

a mother. He ought to have done a three-day course at my place to help him understand that. I read through my letter several times. I was really choked up by it. Because I was saying goodbye to her as if I'd never see her again. Then I went downstairs, because it would soon be time. I imagined a complete volume of my correspondence, and the first letter, the first page, would be this same letter I'd just written, to say a last goodbye to Madame Morozvitch.

There was no one in the bar. But from what little I'd seen there was never anyone in this bar. The TV was on. I asked the barman for something to drink. To my mind, I could have anything I wanted. Seeing they'd already swiped my card when I arrived. They had no reason to be suspicious. So as soon as I asked for something, they agreed without wondering if I was swindling them or something. The only thing they wanted from me was a quick signature. No problem. That's the reason I could even have the most expensive things. Like my bottle just now. I imagined the impression it would make on Mathilde. While I waited I asked for an apricot juice, because that's what I prefer. He gave me a knowing smile, the waiter. And I stayed there, at the bar. I couldn't wait for her in my room, obviously. That was a bit much. The technique was to meet here in the bar and then discuss what she wanted to do for the evening. I regretted not buying an *Officiel des Spectacles* to find out what the cinemas were showing. Okay, but we just had to go and look. There were usually hundreds of films starting round about ten o'clock. We'd see when we got there. And besides, maybe she wouldn't want to go to a movie.

Eight forty-six.

The guy brought my juice. But in the end I asked for a glass of champagne as well. To tell you the truth, champagne, I didn't love it. What I really liked, on the other

hand, was the idea of drinking it. It was impressive, I think. But as a rule I hardly ever drank it. I preferred apricot juice or wine. Beer, I couldn't stand. Anyway, I sipped my juice. The friendly guy gave me a small dish of cocktail snacks. And I asked him where the nearest cinemas were. He told me the best thing was to go to Odéon. There, film-wise, you were basically sorted. After that I wondered if actually she wouldn't prefer to go to a restaurant. Just so we could have dinner tête-à-tête. In that case I'd need to think of somewhere smart. Definitely not a pizza sort of thing. More the type where they get you to taste the wine before pouring you a glass. That, that's style, I think. But it would have most likely bored her. A film was better. Besides, it was dark in there. Afterwards we'd have walked back in the night. And I'd have suggested we have a last glass of champagne in my room. Perhaps she'd hesitate, for form's sake, and because she's a girl. So I'd tell her right away that it wouldn't commit her to anything, that it was just to be with her a bit longer, and so she'd say yes.

On the TV there was one load of rubbish after another: commercials, and then the weather, and then yet more things of no interest. I've always wondered who they are, the millions of people who gawp at TV every night. What I think, me, is that judging from what you see on TV, housewives are brain-dead. I swear to you: brain-dead. For example, there's that advert where a girl tells you she put this skin cream on and that since then her face had really changed. You definitely have to be a moron to believe that. Seeing you can bet that the girl, she'd never heard of the cream before she did the advert. It's just she was offered a lot of money to tell that to the housewife. So the housewife straightway thinks: if this girl says so, then it must be true. And she buys the cream that week to bung all over her face.

Except that her face, it still looks like a housewife's face. There isn't a cream that'll change that. That's obvious. So of course when you see the girl on TV telling you that since she's used this cream she looks ten years younger, you think that they really must take housewives for idiots on the TV. But actually you think they're probably right, seeing they must have done research all over the place to know what they needed to say. In a word, it's depressing. I switched my mobile on again. Always the same little anxiety in my stomach. There wasn't a message. That was really reassuring. If something had cropped up, Mathilde would have let me know. But given the time she must have been on her way by now. So there was no longer any risk she'd call it off. I regretted not having asked for her mobile number. I'd have sent her a text. While I waited I played around with my phone to change the ringtone, which was really dire.

Then I heard the ding of the main door. I got up. She was coming. It was time.

Unfortunately it wasn't her, but a man who came straight into the bar, greeted the barman and sat at a table by the window. The waiter switched off the TV and put on some music instead. A sort of jazz. Then after that he straightway poured a large glass. Me, I think it was whisky. He took it over to the man who'd just come in. From looking at him, the man, I had the feeling I'd seen him somewhere before. He seemed sad. Given the scenario, I thought he was a regular and that he always drank the same thing every time. That was convenient, so the waiter didn't even need to ask him what he wanted any more.

"Another?" he asked me.

In the meantime I'd finished my glass of champagne without realizing. The waiter wanted to give me another.

I thought it best not to. Although I can hold my drink. But I'd had virtually nothing to eat all day. So I said no thanks. After that the waiter, he leant on the bar, to get closer to me sort of thing, and as he could see I was interested in the guy at the other side of the room, seeing I'd done nothing but stare at him for the last few minutes, he started talking to me about him. And he told me something pretty staggering, I think. From what he said, the guy was called Monsieur Elme. He came in every evening and stayed really late. But more than that, he downed an unbelievable amount of whiskies. His technique for knowing when to stop was that when he finished a glass he took a photo from his inside jacket pocket. He looked at it for a long time. And then he either asked for another glass or he went home. So obviously, me, I asked who it was in the photo. And the waiter looked pleased, because that was exactly the question he wanted me to ask. He explained that him too, he'd asked himself that question, and one day he'd asked the guy straight out, who it was in the photo that he always stared at between drinks. And the bloke had told him: "It's a photo of my wife. When I think she's beautiful I go home".

That still made him laugh, the waiter. But I couldn't work out if it was a joke he'd have come out with about any customer, or if it was actually the truth. But to be honest I didn't give a damn basically. Me, what I was worried about was that Mathilde still wasn't there. So I got up. I had the feeling that if I stayed there, in the bar, the waiter would keep on telling me stories like that, and I wasn't in the mood for it. That's why I went back upstairs.

In my room I started reading *Entrevue* again. It was nine fifteen. But after all, it was normal for her not to be here yet.

Fifteen minutes late, you couldn't call that late. Especially not for a girl. She must be caught in traffic, if she'd taken a taxi. Or held up on the métro, if she'd taken the métro. Or she was busy searching the area for the hotel. Perhaps I ought to have arranged to meet her somewhere easier to find. Because it was true that this hotel, it was really tiny and not easy to spot. On the outside I wasn't even sure if it said: '*Hôtel du quai Voltaire*'. So, obviously.

I looked at my bottle of champagne. The ice in the bucket had virtually all melted by now. I took a lump and swallowed it. More and more I had stomach ache. The best thing would have been to have something to eat. But even so, I was really surprised I wasn't hungry. The truth, which I'd rather not have told you, but it was part of the story, is that I was mega-nervous at the thought of being in this room with Mathilde. I was afraid of being awkward and not correct. All of a sudden my mobile rang. It crushed my heart. I thought: no, no, no … I was so afraid she'd cancel. The caller withheld their number. I thought it was better not to answer. In case it was someone I didn't want to talk to. Like my mother or François … Nervously I waited for the beep telling me there was a message, but there wasn't one. No message. That got me in a terrible state. What if it was Mathilde? Why hadn't she left a message? I started walking round and round the room. Fuck. There was something in amongst all this that I wasn't aware of. I told myself that this call, it must have been my mother again or something, and that I ought not to worry. Mathilde wouldn't be long. From what she'd told me, she'd gone shopping with her father. She must have had to find an excuse for coming to meet me. So obviously she might have been held up slightly. But she was going to come. Besides, why wouldn't she come? After all, she'd held my hand at the Jardin

d'acclimatation. So she'd come. All I had to do was wait. I regretted not having a TV. A hotel room with no TV is like a woman with no legs: there's something missing. Even if there's nothing on TV but idiots. It helps pass the time. So I opened the window, and leant out to try and see if she was coming down the street. The embankments were jammed solid. Nothing was moving at all. Apart from the taxi rank, where there was no one. The cars were bumper to bumper. And to put my mind at rest I told myself it could be that her father was going to drop her off by car. But they were late because of the traffic. For example, they'd been shopping at Galleries Lafayette, and when it got to about half-past eight she'd asked him to drop her off in the area. But obviously at this time of night, given the traffic, it took a lot longer than half-an-hour to get to the quai Voltaire. Then I imagined that one day there ought to be a quai Parme somewhere in Paris. That would be good. On Sunday morning people would go for a walk there, reciting some of my poems off by heart. Voltaire, I don't much like him, me. Madame Thomas had got us to read stuff by him. It was okay. But nothing to write home about. In my opinion, a book is worth writing home about when you get a lump in your throat from reading it. And this lump in your throat might be anguish, or sadness, or some other emotion that isn't a nice soft cushion that you sit on to make yourself more comfortable. I know what I mean.

Opposite, on the Seine, there were no more barges going past. It was probably too late. I used to know a girl, her uncle actually lived on a barge. Not in Paris, but somewhere nearby. One time she'd had a sort of party on board. I was trying to focus on all these memories so as not to think about Mathilde too much. The way I see it, waiting for someone who isn't coming is the worst kind of torture. I

tried to remember the girl's name. And also the names of the people I was with at the time. The thing with my mother was that we moved quite a lot. So I often changed schools. That's the reason I don't really have any childhood friends. Then I tried to visualize every apartment I'd lived in. And then I came back to the idea that it was probably too late to see a barge go past. I don't know why, but I wanted to see one. Although it's not something you'd call exceptional, a barge. But I wanted to. Don't ask me why. Then I thought about all the gulls that were taken in by following the barges from Le Havre all the way to Paris. To start with they thought they were onto a good thing. Because no doubt there was plenty to eat on a barge. They had a feast. So obviously they followed the barges for several days. Until they wound up in Paris. And then, I don't know what they did to not be miserable. A seagull, if it hasn't got any sea, it must start to get depressed. Anyway, I was having these kinds of uninteresting thoughts so as not to think about Mathilde, but I couldn't manage it, because the truth is, the only thing I couldn't stop thinking was that she was really late and that maybe she wasn't going to come.

It was almost ten o'clock. One thing was for sure, we were going to miss the last film. But that was no big deal. Going to the cinema wasn't essential, we could give it a miss. I looked in the champagne bucket. The ice was nothing but water now. That was a real blow to my morale. I don't know why. For a moment I came close to calling Marco to ask him for Mathilde's number. Maybe her father hadn't wanted her to go out again after last night's party. But if she didn't call me it was because she intended on coming.

That was for certain. So she was going to come. But she could have phoned to tell me when. So I didn't keep pacing up and down and stressing myself out for no reason. That's why I thought of ringing Marco. But somehow I couldn't see myself talking to him. Not after what he'd done to me. Besides, if I asked him that, within two minutes the whole world would know that Mathilde and I had arranged to meet up this evening. Seeing that Marco was a grass. Who'd screw everything up. Because my mother, she was the type to ring her, Mathilde, and ask where I was. Of course she wouldn't manage to find out, but all the same it annoyed me that they should talk to each other. I could see her now, my mother, telling her what I'd done to Bénédicte. Suddenly that stressed me out. She'd tell her that I'd put her in casualty and that I was violent. At first Mathilde would find it hard to believe. You too, you'd find it hard. To look at me, you wouldn't think I'm the type to hit a girl. Even me, if someone called me one day to say I'd punched a girl in the face, I wouldn't believe them. I'd say: "Sorry old son, that's impossible. I know him inside out, and for good reason, and I'm telling you that that's simply not the way he does things. He's a poet, Julien Parme. A poet, not a thug … " But the problem was that Mathilde would think back to the story about Yann Chevillard which I'd given her in the taxi. She'd also think about the cut on my face. And the blood she'd seen. And she'd start to think I'd been talking a load of rubbish, and that the thing with my stepsister was probably true. And she'd tell herself that I was actually a thick lout, a dangerous guy who was capable of hitting a girl in the face, when a girl's face, it's sacred. Yes, suddenly I thought all that. And I was really frightened that that was what had happened. And that that was the reason she wasn't coming to meet me.

I shut the window. Then I opened it again. And I lit another menthol. I was going to end up getting paranoid. She was going to come. All I had to do was be patient. To pass the time I went into the bathroom. I got some toilet paper and rolled it into balls, and then wet it to make it harder and all soggy, and went back to the window to practise throwing them. It could have been a laugh to try and hit a few passers-by. But it was too risky, I'd be caught within minutes. So what I did was throw them as far as I could. Just to see. Sometimes, when you're waiting for something that doesn't come, you resort to doing stupid things like that. Don't ask me why.

Then suddenly I stopped, on account of another idea I'd had. I thought Mathilde had maybe found out about Madame Thomas and me. I swear to you, the idea sent an awful shudder right through me. How could she have heard about it? Marco, he wouldn't have said anything. It would show me in too good a light. And if there was one thing he didn't like, Marco, it was showing other people in a good light. Especially not me. On the other hand, I could imagine that girl Alice ringing her friend Émilie Fermat to give her grief for not having waited for us. And then obviously she'd have told her how she finished her evening and everything. And you could bet your bottom dollar she'd have talked about me. Girls, I know what they're like. When they talk about something they can't help going into detail. It's too much for them. Especially as this gave her something spicy to tell her. About how I was sleeping with my French teacher, and how on top of that I'd touched her breasts in the taxi. So straight away, Émilie, she'd have repeated it to Mathilde. It would have really put her off me.

I picked up the room phone. I pressed the button to call reception. And I asked the guy if by chance there was

someone waiting for me in the bar. He said he'd go and check, I got my hopes up again, but he came back and said no. That was all I needed. So I asked him to call me in my room if anyone asked for me. He said of course. And we hung up. The thing was that now I felt like being sick. I went to the bog. I even crouched over it, if you want the details. In case. But in the end I didn't feel like it enough. All I managed to do was spit. So I lay on the bed again and glanced through *The Life and Times of Scrooge McDuck*. As I'd finished the big adventure in the middle, I made a start on a story with Mickey. But Mickey, me, I don't like the look of him.

Then I got this terrible intuition, which made me put the magazine down I was so incapable of concentrating on the crappy story: Bénédicte had maybe recognized Mathilde's bag when we ran into each other in Titan's stable. And anyway, Titan, it was Mathilde who'd been riding him just before our argument. In short, she'd maybe worked out why I'd come to the club. Because you could bet she must have spent hours trying to figure out the reason I'd showed up there, at the club. And she must have told herself it was because of Mathilde. That was for sure. I even thought that maybe they knew each other really well, the two of them. Mathilde obviously hadn't realised that our parents lived together. After all, her and me, we didn't have the same name. Her, she was Bénédicte de Courtois. How could she have made a connection with me? Julien Parme. It could be that they often saw each other on Saturday at the club. Sometimes they went for a ride together, and afterwards while they were brushing down their horses, they told each other what was going on in their lives. Friends, like.

Bénédicte was slightly older. I could just see her giving her some advice, particularly when it came to competitions and everything. I couldn't get over it. As I thought about it, this version of events took hold in my mind. And so then Bénédicte would have rung Mathilde to tell her what sort of a lout and little bastard I was, and she'd let herself be convinced. I'd told her a load of rubbish, she realised that now. My story about Yann Chevillard, it was nothing but a ginormous lie. And suddenly she understood that I was a violent guy and the only thing I was interested in was being in a hotel room with her.

That's why she'd decided not to come and meet me. I frightened her. She hadn't even thought to let me know. And so it went on in my mind. It churned away in all directions. I could foresee every possibility, and it made me ill. At one point I even imagined she'd have coughed up the address of my hotel. I was afraid I wasn't safe in my room any more. The cops would have questioned her and she'd have told the truth. As proof, she'd kept the hotel writing paper I'd given her so she'd have my address. I began making up whole films. It could be that they'd turn up any minute. I went back to the window to see. I began to panic. Perhaps it was a good idea to leave the hotel right away. I swear to you, I seriously thought about it. I'd never been so nervous. Because I hadn't the slightest idea where I could go from here. Yet possibilities, there were loads of them. I could change hotels. There was no lack of them in Paris. But I didn't want to. The very idea that Mathilde could have betrayed me, that knocked me flat. I didn't want anything any more. If I got caught here it was because she'd betrayed me, and if she'd betrayed me then I wouldn't have had the guts to go on the run or anything anyway. I'd come quietly. I wouldn't have been

difficult. The cops would have knocked at the door, and I'd have let myself be taken away without a word. I'd have kept quiet, holding out my hands so they could put the cuffs on. And I knew what to expect after that. They'd have taken me down to the station, where I'd have had to tell them everything. Then perhaps they'd have sent me to see a social worker or something, and they'd have asked me to tell them everything again. It would have lasted for hours. And in the end they'd have sent me somewhere. To a boarding school. Or to a special psychiatric centre for individuals like me who have behavioural problems and get up to all sorts of things because of it.

I got up, and I was sick in the bog. It made me burn all over. And then I began to blub. I swear to you. I didn't know why I was crying. It was the acid taste in my mouth which made me snap. And tiredness as well. Afterwards I gave my face a quick wash. I cleaned my teeth, but without enthusiasm. Then I went to bed. I thought about the seagulls again, wondering how they could live in Paris. It made me think about the duckling at the Jardin d'acclimatation. I remembered what Mathilde had said. I should never have picked it up. So I imagined myself getting up. Taking a taxi back there. At the dead of night. Once I got to the entrance, I'd have climbed over the railings. Being very careful. Seeing there's quite a lot of surveillance equipment in the area. Once I was inside I'd have started to run. But behind me, a light would have come on in the darkness. A kind of torch. The security guard's. And I'd have made off as fast as I could. And a chase would have begun all round the park. Luckily I'd have managed to shake him off. But only just. And so then I'd have been able to find the place where I'd seen the little duckling. It would have been hard to find him in the dark.

I'd have the hotel matches with me, and I'd have struck dozens of them, whispering "duckling, duckling" before I found him. I'd have picked him up, very gently, intending to take him back with me and look after him. But then I'd have discovered that he didn't look like anything any more. Or like an old sock. As if he'd been attacked by another duck. By his mother, maybe. In any case, one thing was for certain: he'd be dead. Already dead.

I started to yawn. It must have been eleven o'clock. I was exhausted. I hadn't realised quite how knackered I was. I even found it hard to keep my eyes open. I didn't get undressed. In case Mathilde showed up. For a moment I imagined that her father wouldn't let her go out again. After all, she'd gone to bed after two o'clock the night before. She'd have pretended to do as she was told and go to bed just after dinner. But in fact she'd have got a small bag ready with a few essentials in it. I could imagine her taking a book with her too. That was her style. A novel perhaps. Then she'd do a bunk. By then it would be midnight. Once she was outside she'd have got a taxi to where I was. She'd have been afraid I was already asleep. At reception she'd have asked for my room number. She'd have come up. And then I'd have heard her little fingertips tapping on the door. This version, it was more like her after all. Because Mathilde, it was her who'd held my hand at the fairground, wasn't it. It was her who'd told me the story about her sister running away to cheer me up. Yes, her little fingertips on my door. I had to stay dressed. Just in case. Even if I knew full well she wouldn't come. And that maybe I'd never see her again in my life. Never.

With that I fell asleep.

6

I GOT UP QUITE EARLY. I straightway switched on my mobile. It was nine-thirty. I'd got another message from my mother. This time I listened to it. Her voice was peculiar. She said she was with Bénédicte in casualty, and I'd be well advised to be at home when she got back. It was from yesterday evening. No news from Mathilde on the other hand. Straight after that I went and had breakfast. I'd never eaten quite like it. I told them at reception that I was probably going to stay an extra night. But it wasn't true. Back in my room I got my stuff together. I didn't have a whole lot. I took my magazines. I didn't want to leave them behind for people to find. I put the letter to Madame Morozvitch in an envelope. That would make her happy. Before leaving the room I took a last look round. The sight of the bottle of champagne in its bucket made me depressed.

I went straight to the Gare de Lyon. At first I wanted to go by bus, because the weather was really good, but it was Sunday, and buses on a Sunday, they're like women you love: you can wait for them forever. So I took the métro. As I was a bit early I walked round the station. Then I went and bought a ticket to Rome. The fact of having it in my hand, that ticket, it did something for me. I swear to you. It was for definite now, I'd be able to get away. In the newsagents I wanted to get some magazines. But in the end I went for a novel. They sold tons of them. I thought it wasn't necessarily a masterpiece. Generally speaking, novels they sell at railway stations, they're pretty much

239

railway station novels, if you see what I mean. Badly-written stuff. But still. I wanted one to read. After much deliberation I got *Steppenwolf* by Herman Hesse. Because of the title. I bought a stamp and went looking for a letterbox. Eventually I found one, but I hesitated. After all, could she still read, Madame Morozvitch? Reading, it's never very easy for blind people. But I've already told you that in my opinion, her dark glasses, they were dubious. In the worst case someone would read it to her, like I used to with her son's letters. Maybe it would be her son who'd read it to her. It was a blow to my moral, thinking all that. I didn't want people to know I was going to Italy. Especially not that schmuck. I stood where I was in front of the letterbox for a few minutes, and in the end I threw my letter in the bin. Then I went and looked at the departures board. The train for Lausanne was on platform twelve. Once I got to Lausanne I had five hours to wait, and then I took a couchette to Rome. Couchettes, they're great. Ever since I was small I've loved them. Just sleeping on a train gives you the impression of going a very long way. Before making my way to platform twelve I sat outside a café just across from the platforms. I wanted an apricot juice but they didn't have any. So I made do with orange juice. I watched the people going past. Most of them were about to leave. They were dragging gigantic suitcases. I also saw a guy with skis. That surprised me in April. But apparently some mountains are so high that you can ski all year round. It was my father who'd told me that. And other people had often said it since. So it must be true.

I had almost two hours' wait ahead of me. I started reading the novel. It was really good. At the beginning it was the story of a guy who's split in two: he was both a wolf and a man. Herman Hesse, it was the metaphor

he'd used to denote madness. Because in fact his problem, the hero's, was that he was mad. And every time he did something, the wolf inside him bared its teeth. And every time the wolf inside him drove him to do certain things, the man reproached himself and regretted what he'd done. In short, there was a permanent conflict within him. Then the hero met a girl in a jazz bar. She was full of life and everything. What proved it was that along with music, what she loved was dancing. It was her who'd reconciled him with life. That's what the novel was about. For a change I thought it was amazing. Especially the writing. And what it said about life. In my opinion, Voltaire ought to have read it before he started writing his silly stories.

I thought about Mathilde again. I couldn't understand why I hadn't heard from her. It was really a mystery. Again I searched through all the possibilities in my mind, although with exhaustion. In fact it was like the empty office where the light was on all night: no matter how hard you searched for explanations, drew up theories, you couldn't find a single one that would let you say once and for all: "It's this" or: "It's that". In any case one thing was for sure, and that was that she'd stood me up. But at the same time, when you think about it, she hadn't given anyone the address of my hotel. She could have done. Some people would have. That, it would have been awful. But no. She'd respected that. Maybe at this very moment she was at her bedroom window, at her father's place. She was looking at the view, the one she'd shown me. Opposite, the light in the office was switched off. And she was saying to herself that I must be at the station and that I was about to leave for Italy. She was imagining me like this, outside a café, thinking of her, and of the train I was going to catch any minute. As for Italy, she was the only one who knew about it. And

she must have been thinking that at her bedroom window. That it was our secret. With that thought, I realised I was happy. And at ease. I can't explain why. Deep down, I told myself, she didn't totally betray me. She was hoping I was aware of that. Something had happened to stop her from coming to meet me, but she was hoping I'd understand it wasn't a betrayal. Not really.

Then immediately I began dreaming about Italy. For ten minutes I reread the same page of the novel. I'd disappeared into my thoughts. I had enough cash for the next few days. After that, I'd sort something out. I'd find something, obviously. And if I didn't find something then I'd get on a train for Nice. I'd explain everything to my uncle. He'd understand. In short, life went on. You'd almost think that it was now that it was beginning. Life. I'd had trouble ridding myself of all my problems, but now it had got off to a start. I looked up from my book. To the right was a gigantic clock. The train was leaving in ten minutes. But I preferred to wait until the last moment before getting up. And so I went back to reading.

The part I was trying to finish was fantastic. The hero met a Spanish musician who gave him some cigarettes, but ultra-special ones which enabled him to go off into a state of total delirium within himself. Once you'd smoked it, this drug, you found yourself in a kind of long corridor with lots of doors. And behind each door was something to help reconstruct your personality. At one point the hero actually met Mozart, whom he worshipped. Me, for example, if I could have gone down that corridor, I'm sure that on the other side of one of the doors I'd have come face to face with La Fontaine. We could have had a little literary natter. In peace and quiet, between friends. I'd have told him that, frankly, since he died, no one had written anything as good

as the *Fables*, and that we'd studied them this year with Madame Thomas. He'd have listened to me attentively. He's an attentive guy, La Fontaine. Then he'd have offered me something to drink. Tea, that sort of thing. Or some apricot juice. Because you can bet it's his favourite juice as well. And then suddenly, just as I was in the middle of talking to him about the novel I wanted to write, which was called *Apricot Juice*, he'd have asked me if I was intending on catching it, the train to Rome.

"Why?"

Then he'd have taken a clock out from under his shirt. Straight up, a clock. I know as a rule that that's impossible. But this was La Fontaine. The greatest of all writers. Okay. And on the clock you could clearly see that there were only three minutes before my train upped and left.

"I know, I know ... " I'd have replied, laid-back. It was time to go. But what he was unaware of, Jean, was just how fast I can run. Between the tortoise and the hare, me, there's no doubt about it: to get from the café where I'm sitting daydreaming to platform twelve would take me less than a minute. So I'd still got two left. And when you've dreamt of meeting La Fontaine all your life, two minutes extra, that's really something. So he'd have asked me to go for a little stroll with him. A quick one. And he'd have taken me by the arm. Just between writers. We'd have walked like that along the great corridor, discussing animals. Then we'd have stopped outside a door. What was behind it, I hadn't a clue. So he told me to open it and see. Okay. I did so. And then I found myself in a strange room, white all over. Bénédicte was lying on a bed with tubes coming out of her everywhere. A nurse came up to me and explained that she'd been attacked by a herd of elephants. And that she was in a coma.

"In a coma?" I straightway replied. "But it can't be, we only had a little argument, that's all. She must be putting it on. I know her. She's a bitch. She always puts things on to make you feel guilty."

"No no ... I'm telling you she's in a coma. A mild coma, but even so ... a whole herd of elephants went over her."

So I turned to Jean to find out what he thought about it, but he'd disappeared. I called to him: "Jean! Jean!" But no one replied. It really nauseated me to stay in that depressing room. So I went back into the corridor, but I still couldn't find him. I was panic-stricken. I started running around in all directions. All the doors in the corridor were locked. Except one. I opened it. You should have seen me, my heart was in my boots. You could hear a loudspeaker shouting really loud: 'More than a minute! More than a minute!' I knew it was talking about my train. But I pretended not to understand. Anyway. I opened the door. It was the one to my apartment, I recognized it immediately, and I came across my mother. I thought back to the story Mathilde had told me about her sister running away. When she'd come back, her father had run into her arms and told her, in tears, never to do that to him again. But that wasn't possible for me, on account of Bénédicte who was maybe in a coma. So I really started to kick myself for having hit her. I'd have liked to turn the clock back. But it was too late. What's done is done. Besides, that's one reason why life is a trap that we all end up falling into eventually.

On the main concourse of the Gare de Lyon, I looked up from my novel. I'm crazy, I thought. Completely crazy. Every time I read I go off into a world of my own, and I read the same page umpteen times. The train was leaving any minute but I couldn't tear myself away from my book. There were still ten pages left. I began reading again. 'I

must finish it before I catch the train, I must', I thought. It was the first time I'd read a whole book in one go. Ten pages, it's not a huge amount, except every page was an excuse to daydream. But I concentrated hard so I could finish it as quickly as possible. I saw myself already, on the last word, getting up and running off, running, a hare I'm telling you, and boarding the train a second before the door shut. I'd sit down in my seat and it would take at least ten minutes to get my breath back and for my heart to stop racing. I'd press my face to the window and I'd watch the scenery go by, slowly at first and then faster and faster. That would do something for me. *Goodbye cruel world*, I'd say in my mind. But quite emotional, all the same. Sitting opposite me, maybe there'd be a really beautiful Swiss girl who was going skiing in the mountains with their everlasting snows and everything. I'd reel off a few of La Fontaine's fables to impress her. The one about the frog who wanted you to think he was as big as a cow for example. After four hours chatting she'd fall under my spell and she'd suggest I spend a few days with her and her family in the Alps. You never know, that sort of thing, it can happen. Or I'd stay there, face against the window, gazing at the suburbs of Paris, then at the countryside. With fields full of sheep, and farms. And at last I'd feel life taking root in me. Real life.

I put down my book. I got up without hurrying. The train was long gone by now. I left some money for my apricot juice. I had my ticket in my hand. I looked at it. I also looked at the empty platform across the way. For a moment I stood there, not moving, thoughtful and solemn, like a mountaineer who's reached the summit of Mont Blanc,

but who knows his destiny is to ultimately go back down again.

Then I turned on my heel. I walked out of the station. I took a taxi. During the drive I began to cry, although only a little. I'd got stomach ache. And my tears, as they ran down onto my cut, they stung really badly. But I told myself that it was so much the better, that I deserved it, and I even dug my nails into my wrists so it would hurt even more. I thought about my father.

I thought about him for a long time.

Then, when I arrived at my building, I got out of the taxi. I dried my eyes. I put in the door code. Here I was then. I went into the entrance hall, I was trembling to the depths of my being. To give myself courage I thought of the story Mathilde had told me about her sister. I imagined my mother the same way, putting her arms round me, crying, and asking me never to do that to her again. If this miracle were to happen, one thing's for certain: I wouldn't ever do it again. Not ever. I'd learn how to live my life and to behave properly. I wouldn't tell any more lies.

I took a deep breath to drive away my fears. And I got into the lift, hoping very much that she'd forgive me. That she'd forgive me for being who I am, and not someone else.

D1339315

C014940802